SILENCE

ZI TRONE

THE WHUMPY PRINTING PRESS

To my friend Mill, who has always supported me.

CONTENTS

Content Warnings

This story contains the following content:
- Institutionalised/systemic pet whump

- Dehumanisation

- Past abuse and trauma

- Medical whump

- Forced medical treatment

- Morally dubious caretaker

- Defiant whumpee

If this book isn't for you, no worries! But if it is, we hope you enjoy this story about a runaway pet...

STRAY DOG

It had been days since the first time Rayan had heard the rustling from behind the big, green dumpster. It was in an alley close to his apartment, frequented by many of the strays he'd helped over the years – cats, dogs, you name it. He just loved the little guys, and when he had enough money to spare, he liked to bring them little treats until they trusted him enough that he could bring them to a shelter. He'd even found loving homes for some of them around the neighbourhood, and seeing the scared, sopping wet dogs he had fed from his palm prance around on the streets in a little dog-coat and with a smiling owner ... that always warmed his heart.

In that first phase of trying to build trust, he never stuck around to wait and see what came to the bowl, allowing the strays peace and quiet. Some privacy. He knew from experience that was the best way to approach them, especially the cats, and there was a big chance this newest one was a cat. The bowl was always empty by the time he came back, and he was glad to see that his cat-and-dog-safe paste mixture was to the liking of the little critter. It was important to make it into a paste; he'd learned that the hard way. Some of these animals' teeth were a complete mess, and they couldn't really eat solids.

After a week or so, he decided to stay as he presented the mystery animal with yet another bowl full of food and another bowl of clean water. He really hoped it would still come out of hiding despite his presence, at least so he could see what he was dealing with.

"Here, love. I've brought you some food," he said softly, stepping away from the bowl to give it space. He crouched down and waited, eyes surveying the alleyway curiously.

Soon enough, he heard that signature rustling, and something poked its head out from behind the dumpster.

That wasn't a cat. It wasn't even a dog.

He watched in astonishment as the thin and dirty little thing crawled out of the shadows and dragged itself over to the bowl, eyeing him warily. Neither of them said a word. Maybe this poor guy hadn't talked to anyone in ages and didn't know what to say. Rayan was simply too stunned to.

It was a pet. An actual pet, the kind that looked awfully similar to people, with a worn, black collar around its neck and an expression that told Rayan it was not happy that he decided to stay.

Rayan had never seen a pet up close like this before. He had learned about them in school, he had seen some famous, rich people's pets, he had studied the rules and laws regarding them extensively, wanting to adopt one someday. With all that knowledge neatly tucked into the crevices of his brain, he should've been way more prepared and way less like a kid staring at a monkey in a zoo with their mouth hanging open.

"Sorry I'm not a dog," it spat, making him snap out of it.

"Oh ... no, that's not – if I'd known – "

"You wouldn't have brought me anything. I know."

"No! I would've brought you normal food! On a plate!"

It still seemed full of distrust, probably for good reason. Who knew how other people must've been treating it up until now? Strays were a rare occurrence when it came to pets, and the ones that ran away usually had a damn good reason to.

Rayan reached towards the bowl, making the other pull it closer protectively, glaring at him. "I'm not trying to – it must be disgusting! Let me bring you real food instead, please."

"Then bring it. I'll finish this by the time you come back."

He sighed and stood up. "Okay. I'll be right back, then."

On his way back to the apartment, Rayan couldn't help but wonder why the poor pet decided to show itself if it thought a dog would've been more appreciated – to the point where it thought it was risking its only source of food by not being one. It must've heard his voice and known he was still there, right?

He grabbed a plate and stacked some food onto it from the fridge. He decided to heat up some instant ramen too, hoping the warm soup would help combat the chill. Logically, he should've called the Pet Protection Agency to take care of the poor stray. The pet probably knew this. Did it think Rayan was somehow different? If it did, Rayan supposed it was right, because his thoughts were nowhere near the possibility of making that phone call.

The only thing he could think of as a logical explanation was that under all that snark and cynicism, it wanted to be found and cared for. Of course it did. It was a pet, it needed to be cared for. But maybe, because of some odd turn of events, it might've wanted to be cared for outside of the system, by someone other than its legal owner. But why? It should've been having a blast at its owner's. The PPA was supposed to ensure a happy life for all pets, right? If it *wasn't* having a blast, it should've been taken away and given to someone better.

In any case, throwing itself at the mercy of another was most likely easier to bear if it acted like it wasn't hoping for even a scrap of kindness. Like it already knew it'd be rejected, so there was no way to surprise it.

Rayan was determined to do so anyway. To shock it with just how much he already cared, after days of no contact and a five-minute encounter.

Sil

Rayan sat on the ground a few feet away from the stray as it ate. He was lost in thought, quietly observing the visible injuries and weird bumps under its skin. Bones healed wrong, maybe.

The more he thought about this entire situation, the more he found himself absolutely furious with the pet's previous owner. He had wanted a pet his entire life. He had grown up wanting one, seeing how happy and lively and perfect they were, knowing that if he was just a little more fortunate, worked just a little harder, got out of his one-bedroom dwelling and moved into something a tiny bit more spacious, *maybe* the Pet Protection Agency would consider him as a potential adopter. He had always been so passionate about wanting to give poor, helpless things a better life; that was precisely why he was so obsessed with helping the stray cats and dogs around the area. His ultimate goal was to get one of the pets out of a shelter and give it a loving home, the best home he possibly could.

And then there were people like this guy's owner. He couldn't fathom having the wealth and opportunity to adopt a pet and then treating it like utter garbage. He couldn't fathom how the PPA could've given someone like that a licence in the first place. Wasn't there an interview? Weren't they supposed to check up on pets regularly? How did they miss this?

His new acquaintance put down the cup gently, almost like it was handling expensive glass or something. Quite out of character for someone moving around so jerkily, and who had pretended not to care much for the soup in the first place.

"My name's Rayan. May I ask what your name is?" He kept his voice quiet, both so he could avoid startling it and so others on the street wouldn't hear.

"Wouldn't we both like to know?" It choked out a dry laugh, devoid of any joy or amusement. "Owner called me *mutt*, or *that thing*. I'm not sure I ever had a name, *Rayan*." His name felt like an insult coming from the pet, as if he was in the wrong for simply having one when it didn't.

Rayan frowned. "Well, do you wanna have one? You could give me anything. Make something up. Go back and change it later if you come up with something better ... Surely, you don't want me to call you those things?"

"Why do you need to call me anything?" it snapped suddenly. "You're making it sound like you'll just stick around and humour me forever! Why don't you go on your way already?"

"I – well ... " Rayan rubbed the back of his neck anxiously, awkwardly, looking for words that wouldn't upset the other. He wasn't sure words like that existed. "I was hoping I'd find you here tomorrow, like ... like always. Well, for the past week. And that I'd have a name to call you by when I came back."

The stray's eyes narrowed in suspicion, but it didn't lash out again. In fact, it didn't react at all, which was already better than the outburst a moment ago. Rayan counted it as a win.

"Think about it, okay?" he said with what he hoped was a friendly and pleasant smile. "I'll take this stuff back now. I'll bring you more tomorrow, if ... you know, if you're still here. If I didn't annoy you into leaving and finding another place."

He slowly inched closer and grabbed the bowls and the plate with the cup on it, still without getting a single word in response. It was only when he turned to leave that he heard a quiet voice from behind him, so unlike the harsh tone he had just gotten used to.

"I've been calling myself Sil. In my head. I was always told to be silent, so I guess I just took it and ran with it."

Rayan stopped and glanced back at the stray, *Sil*, nodding his understanding without giving any indication that he noticed the faint blush on its face. "Sil it is, then."

"Will you really come back tomorrow?" it asked, prompting him to fully turn back around. "Am I really worth it, compared to a dog?"

"Hey." Rayan crouched down to be at eye level with it. "I'll be back, as long as you want me to. You could even come home with me." Sil visibly recoiled at the idea, and he quickly added,

"It's just an option. Just letting you know. All I'm saying is I'll be back tomorrow. For sure."

"Okay," it said quietly, watching Rayan stand up again with those sharp eyes that seemed to catch even the smallest of movements. The eyes of someone that had been hurt by those movements.

"See you tomorrow, Sil."

DISTRUST

The next day, Rayan was considerably more nervous as he made his way to the alley. He used to be excited, sure, wanting to find out what was hiding in there ... but now he *knew*. And he had no idea whether it would still be there.

"Sil?" He didn't put the plate down this time, wanting to hand it to the pet instead. Sil poked its head out from behind the dumpster, seemingly disapproving of this new idea.

"Do I need to do tricks for it now?" it groaned. "Roll over? Sit pretty?"

"What? No, I – "

Rayan averted his gaze, knowing that at the core of it, that was what he'd had in mind. He wanted to lure it closer, build some more trust. He was still treating it like a stray dog, when pets were so entirely different.

"I'm sorry." He put down the plate of food, stepping back. "I won't force anything. Like, in exchange for food. You don't have to earn it, is what I'm trying to say."

Sil began carefully moving towards it, never taking its eyes off of him. Now that Rayan could see it a little better and knew what to look for, it was obvious that it was in pain. The way it compensated for loss of movement in some areas, the way it winced when it made a wrong move ... He was sure that part of it moving so slowly was caution, but the other part was definitely the pain.

Rayan had no idea how to approach the topic of a vet's visit, and it ended up causing him a long, sleepless night. He thought he'd just grab a stray animal, bring it to the vet, and be done with it. But Sil ... he couldn't just put it into a box. Then there was the issue of the licence. Only licensed pets could be brought to a vet, and they took the rules *very* seriously. The moment he showed up with an unregistered pet, they would take it away and bring it right back to the sly fucker who managed to avoid questions up until now. He could already picture it. *"Oh, I don't know how it got these injuries. It must've happened in the time it was on the streets. Yes, of course I'll pay for all the treatments, I'm a good owner, see?"*

He couldn't bring in Sil as a pet. But trying to bring it in as a person, trying to trick a doctor, would put all three of them in danger of serious legal trouble. He didn't want to put anyone else in harm's way, and that was precisely why he had decided that when the doctor finally got back to him, he wouldn't mention an in-person visit, only ask some general questions over the phone about things that he himself might be able to do to help.

Unfortunately, said doctor had just found the time to call back.

The ringtone sent Sil scurrying back to its nest, food untouched.

"Oh no – goddammit, why now … ?" He pressed a hand down on his pocket to muffle the music. "It's just my phone, Sil, please eat! I'll just – I'll be right around the corner!" He took a few steps away for privacy and took the call.

***

Sil couldn't stop shaking. The sound of the phone startled it so badly, and the most frustrating thing was that it couldn't even explain why. It wished it had at least grabbed the food before running like a coward.

It could faintly hear Rayan's voice from the street, talking to someone. It couldn't make out a single word from so far away, but it found itself curious enough to shuffle towards the source.

" … They seem hurt … yes, I think so … no, they're just – bumps under the skin, yes … I can't bring them in … it's complicated, I just can't … "

They. Who were *they*? Ah, of course, Rayan must've been talking to a professional or something. He had to pretend he was talking about a person, so he could ask his questions without raising suspicion.

No. That didn't make any sense. That was a pet train of thought, a *stray* train of thought, from someone who had been running from the Agency for almost a year now. From a *person* point of view, all Rayan had to do was call the PPA and have it be brought in. Returned to its owner. That was the 'right' thing to do, wasn't it? He was probably just talking about someone else … with bumps under their skin.

Sil leaned against the cold brick wall. It studied its hand, noting that the weight loss had made the protruding bone even more pronounced. It had been broken by its owner after one of the minor offences it'd committed, and he never ended up taking it to the vet. He never took it anywhere, not even the fundraiser balls or the – the other *stuff* the pets kept getting so well dressed for. It had been hidden away from public view for years, some gross, useless, nameless thing. Master hated it and never *ever* failed to make that known.

Maybe its wrist healed wrong, but was that really important? It could live with the pain, it had for years now. Its ankle and shoulder were honestly way more of an issue for it, the agony of walking getting a little too much as time passed, but even that was negligible. Surely, if even its owner thought that wasn't worth a vet's visit, it couldn't have been a big deal.

It looked up at the grey sky above and let out a small sigh. It had no idea why it had decided to come out with Rayan around. It had spent so long hiding from all the people in all the towns and cities it had passed, and now that it was finally quite far from where its owner was, it had decided to blow its cover and just *trust* that this man – Rayan – would be an ally. That he wouldn't call the authorities. That he would just keep bringing it food and water, that he would keep being kind, that he would keep being so *odd* and *different*.

It wasn't so sure about its decision anymore. It desperately wanted to take it back, so it wouldn't have to sleep with one eye open for when the PPA finally got Rayan's report about the stray behind the dumpster.

Sil poked its head out again, trying to see whether he had come back yet. He hadn't. It crawled over to the plate and brought it back to its hiding spot, stuffing its face as quickly as it could in case he changed his mind about having to earn it. It *wasn't* going to do tricks for food.

***

The doctor had told Rayan dreaded news after dreaded news. In-person visit. Rebreaking of bones. Potential lice and other parasites. Infections. He didn't even know where to start, especially since Sil didn't even want to be near him.

The plate was gone by the time he got back to the alley, and he smiled a little. At least it was eating. "Sil?"

A thin little arm appeared from behind the dumpster, placing the plate on the ground. He frowned. Was it not going to come out again?

"Is everything okay?"

"As much as it's ever been."

"I'm sorry about the phone call. Did I upset you somehow?"

"Does it matter?"

Rayan slowly walked over to where the plate was, resisting the urge to peek behind the trash where Sil's hiding place seemed to be. He backed off with the plate now in his hands, stopping at his regular spot. "It matters to me. If I did, I didn't mean to, and I'm sorry."

"Who were you talking about? On the phone."

"Well ... well, um ... you. I was – I was trying to get you a vet's visit, or at least some advice – "

"You were talking about me like I was a person. I don't like that, and I don't trust that."

He opened and closed his mouth a couple times. How was he going to explain that? *Yeah, that's because I'm trying to sneak you past security and avoid the agency that was founded specifically to protect you, all so that I can take care of you instead of your owner that I've decided is a horrible person.* That didn't sound very trustworthy or morally correct, even in his head. Said out loud, he assumed it would sound even worse.

Still, hiding the truth would be an entirely selfish act. If Sil wanted him to call the Agency, he supposed he had no other choice.

But then again, Sil ran away and was currently hiding behind a dumpster. Surely, it'd understand?

Unless it was lost, and it really had sustained all those injuries on the streets, and he was making horrible assumptions about a potentially very kind owner who was desperately looking for their beloved pet. But a lost pet would've just gone up to an officer, right? To be returned?

Either way, Rayan could only imagine what kinds of people would want to forgo making a report so they could keep an undocumented stray all to themselves, and he was about to come clean about being such a person. Sil had no way of telling that his intentions were actually good.

"I ... I told them you were a person because I didn't want the PPA to get involved. You look very hurt, and I assumed it was from your owner, and that's why you're out here all alone and hiding. I was afraid they'd send you back."

Sil didn't respond, no matter how long Rayan waited. He didn't know what it was thinking. He didn't know whether the answer had made it despise him. He wished he could've scooped it up in his arms and told it that all he wanted was to make it all better, but that was a far cry from where they stood with each other right now.

"I'll bring you a blanket tomorrow, if ... if that's okay. If you're still here. It's getting colder. See you tomorrow, Sil. I hope."

— · —

EMERGENCY

Rayan didn't bring up the vet again, or the offer for Sil to join him in his house. Instead he brought it little pieces of the much dreaded *inside*: sweaters, blankets, warm drinks and soup, trying to coax it further out of its shell. He spent their limited time together talking to it, asking how it was feeling, in Sil's words, 'pretending it was a person'. At this point, Rayan was pretty certain that its owner was just an all-around horrible person. In what world were pets undeserving of a few words of comfort? Well ... in Sil's world, apparently.

It had been easy to forget how cold it was really getting while bundled up in warm coats himself, thinking maybe slow and steady was eventually going to win the race. It had been easy to forget that time was very much of the essence, and one day, he woke up to white skies and snow-covered rooftops.

Rayan didn't immediately register the implications of that. Once again, he was cosy under the blankets, with soft pyjamas and fuzzy socks on his feet. He was still stretching and rolling this way and that when suddenly, something clicked in his head. *Sil.*

He had never put on clothes quicker than he did that morning. He ran outside with his coat half-open, racing to the dumpster that was now all white and icy – and behind it, there it was. Poor, shivering Sil, curled up into the tightest ball of misery and borrowed sweaters. It had made itself a little nest with all the fabric Rayan had previously brought it, but that did very little to keep out the winter chill.

"Oh, Sil ... " He swallowed and looked around, cursing himself for being so careless. He should've been looking at the weather forecast religiously. He should've been more stern! He should've just brought Sil inside when it had begun to get so cold, instead of waiting around to gain its trust so fully. No, he was stupider than that – he was trying to wait until it *asked* to be let inside. Sil was never going to *ask*. He'd thought he was giving it space, but he was doing nothing but letting it turn into a betrayal-flavoured popsicle.

He scooped up the shivering thing into his arms carefully, his heart breaking further when Sil didn't even have the energy to push him away. It groaned quietly, murmuring something that was most likely a protest, but other than that, it seemed to cling more than it was trying to get away.

Rayan walked all the way back to his home and set it down on the couch, biting his lip as he thought back to his first aid classes and the fact that he was going to have to undress Sil. He had tried his best to respect its boundaries, but this just wasn't the time to agonise over that. Maybe Sil would hate his guts forever, but god, he just wanted to make sure it would be around to do that.

He carefully removed all of its wet clothes, piling them on the floor. Upon reaching the collar, he hesitated. Sil had always been fiercely protective over it. He didn't get it – he thought its owner was a bad person, someone deserving of their pet running away from them, but seeing Sil be so adamant about keeping it on, he didn't know anymore. He'd *tried* to understand, but his questions only seemed to annoy the pet.

"*You wanna take it away?*"

"*No, that's not –* "

"*So stop asking. It's none of your business whether I keep it on.*"

He grabbed a clean towel and gently patted Sil down, then left the fluffy thing on top of it while he went to fetch some dry clothes. It felt strange to have a barely conscious pet on his couch, dressed in his own sweater and pants, but he couldn't afford to just stand there and dissect the feeling. He ran back to the bedroom for extra blankets and draped those over it as well, just to be a hundred percent sure it wasn't going to wake up to any sort of cold. Only then did he slip out the front door to retrieve the rest of the blankets from the snow, the ones he couldn't immediately pick up along with Sil.

He considered calling emergency services. In truth, he barely had any idea what he was doing, only relying on something he'd learned in tenth grade along with his driver's ed course. But he knew more about first aid than Sil's predicament. What if he was dooming it by calling them? Because honestly, nothing about this entire thing was adding up in his head.

First of all, how did the PPA not pick up on the abuse Sil had so clearly gone through? There were annual welfare checks for all the pets in Lezune, around the entire damn country, specifically to ensure that cases like this were prevented. But even if prevention failed, the PPA were supposed to pick up on bad situations and remove the pet immediately, revoke the owner's licence, and make it as right as they possibly could. There was a chance that someone had inflicted all of these injuries upon the poor thing in less than the span of a year, before the first check-up was due, and Rayan actually hoped *that* was the case.

Because the other possibility was *bribery*. That was his first thought on the day that he'd met Sil, and while he'd tried to be understanding and go through the information he had with a clear head, he just kept coming back to the same conclusion. A regular owner would've long been jailed for severe neglect and abuse, but some people just had a way with ... words. He supposed the money did most of the talking.

That would also explain why Sil hadn't gone to the authorities to be checked into a shelter. Its chip would've been read, and its owner would've likely figured out a way to get it right back to the same abusive home it had escaped from, rendering all of its efforts useless.

Sil let out a pained moan and Rayan was immediately by its side, kneeling next to the couch and waiting for any sort of request from the pet. "Sil? Uh, try not to freak out, okay? I brought you inside because of the cold, you're in my living room. Do you need anything? A warm drink? Soup?"

"Where's my collar ... " it mumbled.

"Right next to us. Your clothes are here too. I'm gonna wash everything for you, okay?"

"No!" Its eyes snapped open fully, and it turned to Rayan with the most panicked expression he'd ever seen. "No, n-no, please, I need it, please, don't touch my clothes ... Please give back my collar, please ... "

"Hey, hey, calm down – "

"I need it, it's all I have, *please*, give it back!" Sil tried to push itself up, immediately failing with the weight of all those blankets on top of it. Rayan gently pushed it back down onto the couch, hushing it.

"I'll give it back. I'll give it back right now, okay? I'll put it right next to you, but please, don't put it back on. It's all wet and dirty."

"Just give it back," it repeated brokenly, and Rayan quickly snatched the collar up from the floor and laid it right next to its face. Sil seemed to calm down considerably at that, scooting over so it could press its cheek against the leather. It closed its eyes again, breathing a sigh of relief.

"I'm sorry I took it without asking," Rayan said softly as he sat back down on the floor. "I was just trying to get all the wet stuff off of you, so you wouldn't get sick."

"Please don't take my clothes ... " It looked at Rayan pleadingly, and he just didn't have the heart to say no. He could've – he easily could've. Sil was defenceless and weak; it couldn't even get up from the couch without assistance. He could've taken those clothes and ripped them apart right in front of it if he wanted to. He pushed all the horrible, intrusive thoughts away, almost tearing up at the fact that its previous owner might've done quite similar things to it.

"I won't. I promise I won't."

Sil nodded in response, wincing as it tried to turn over and find a more comfortable position. Seeing that, a theory began to form in Rayan's head as to why a runaway pet would just stay in one spot for weeks, aside from the free food. The constant walking and running it must've had to do was likely taking a toll on its battered body. That was probably why it had decided to put all its eggs in one Rayan-shaped basket ... it didn't have a choice anymore. Not with winter approaching.

He stayed right there until Sil drifted off, wondering how any pet could be so extremely loyal to an abusive owner. It was clearly so attached, Rayan couldn't even imagine what must've finally led to it running off, and the subsequent emotional turmoil it must've caused. It must've been a life or death situation to push it over the edge. And for someone to take advantage of that devotion and love, that *trust* … He shook his head and got up, grabbing Sil's clothes and bringing them to the closest possible radiator. Maybe they'd even fully dry by the time the pet woke up, and he could just place them back on the floor where they had been without it noticing a single thing.

He tried to shake out the individual pieces as gently as he could so the sound wouldn't wake Sil, but when he got to the pants, something fell out. Thankfully it landed on the carpet, so even though it seemed like a piece of metal, the noise was barely audible. He put the worn pair of slacks on the radiator and picked up the thing, realising with glee that it was a *name tag*. That was perfect! He could track who the owner was, he just had to read the –

Rayan deflated when he turned it around and saw that the engraving was too scratched up and faded to make out anything. He could see some digits of the facility number, and then a capital B … maybe that was supposed to be Sil's name, then? It seemed too short to be its owner's name. Plus, there was another name right under it, something that resembled his own much more closely. And lastly, maybe a phone number? He couldn't even see the area code.

He sighed and put the trinket on top of the pants, so Sil could find it later; then he thought better of it and slipped it back into the pocket. He had the feeling Sil wouldn't appreciate the fact that he'd tried to read it.

But didn't it say that its owner refused to give it a name? So what was up with that pet name-looking row? Rayan walked back to the couch and sat down on the floor, pulling out his phone and looking up some of the biggest national news outlets, as well as some regional ones. Maybe someone had lost a pet recently. And maybe it was someone whose name fit perfectly into the blanks on that name tag.

GUEST

"Rayan?"

The quiet little voice made Rayan look up from his phone immediately. There wasn't anything interesting on it anyway. No matter where he looked, it seemed there wasn't a single runaway pet within the borders; every pet was happy and right where it was supposed to be, no owner was crying on any social media platforms, and there was no ongoing police investigation. Nothing. To the media, Sil didn't exist.

To Rayan, though, it was the only thing in existence right now.

"What's up?" he asked softly.

"Hurts ... "

He had to admit, Sil did look absolutely miserable. It had barely moved since Rayan brought it inside – granted, it had also spent a lot of that time asleep. When it was awake, it just kept groaning and whining, and now it was looking at him with the most pain-filled, teary eyes that he had ever seen. Its expression was open and vulnerable, a stark contrast to the apparently not-so-permanent scowl he had gotten accustomed to. It was just … jarring. Heartbreaking.

"Can you tell me what hurts? And how? Maybe I can get you medication for it."

"No – no, no, no … no pills … no, please … " It squeezed its eyes shut, shaking its head weakly. "No pills … no … "

"You don't like meds, huh … Bad memories?"

"*No* memories."

Rayan was confused only for a moment before he realised what Sil was so afraid of. Dirucodone. Of course. It must've had a bad experience with the amnesia drug once, and now it didn't want anything to do with medications. "Hey, painkillers aren't gonna make you forget anything. I don't even have access to the amnesia pill, I couldn't give you that if you asked."

A tear trickled down its cheek, onto the fabric of the couch. "No pills," it repeated stubbornly. "I won't – I won't forget … I can't … "

"You love your owner a lot, don't you?" Rayan asked compassionately, further saddened when Sil nodded. "I'm sorry, love. I wish I could reunite you two. And – and I'll try my best to help, but first you have to get better yourself, okay? And for that, please tell me where it hurts. It could be something serious."

"Everywhere … it hurts – it hurts everywhere … it hurts to talk … "

"Does your throat hurt?" Sil nodded. Of course it had caught a cold outside like that. "Okay, I'll ask you some yes or no questions, then. Do you also have a headache?" Nod. "Nausea?" Nod. "Uh ... everywhere ... limb pain? Like, arms and legs? Feeling a little achy?" Nod. "Chest tight?" Nod. "That really is everywhere ... That's bad. But not horrible." He gently put a hand against Sil's forehead, feeling for a fever, and of course, with his luck, it was burning up. "Okay, we're getting into horrible territory. Sil ... I'm gonna need you to take some meds."

"No, no, please!" It tried to scoot farther down on the couch to hide under the blankets, probably jostling some sensitive areas in the process, judging from the whimpers. "Please, please, sir, please, I'm sorry ... "

Rayan didn't even know whether he wanted that title to be a little slip-up indicative of it not being fully there and fully lucid, or just a defence mechanism for when it got too scared to be snarky. Neither of the options were particularly promising. "It's not gonna make you forget, Sil, I promise ... It's just gonna make you feel better. Why don't we start with a little candy that'll make your throat hurt less? Would that be less scary?"

Sil shook its head frantically. "D-doesn't hurt, it doesn't hurt, I'm fine, it doesn't hurt ... "

Okay, they weren't getting anywhere with this. Rayan sighed and backed off a little, trying to think of what would be the best course of action. Was he supposed to let it be? Or was he supposed to force some medication into it in the name of the greater good? At that moment, he really wished he had taken that class on decision-making under pressure.

He had already done quite a lot of things by now to make sure Sil came out on the other side feeling relatively okay, right? Putting his foot down and being a little stern over the medication was just an extension of that same effort ...

Except Sil wasn't fighting anymore, and that was the worst part about all of this. Rayan wasn't going up against that feral alley stray he'd met that first day, he was pestering and tormenting a weak, vulnerable pet. God, he felt so unbelievably awful about this whole thing. He bit his lower lip and stood up, deciding he was going to get those meds in Sil's system by whatever means necessary.

"I'm sorry, I'm sorry, I'm sorry ... " Rayan muttered while getting all the medication together: one for the fever, one for the cold, a painkiller, and a throat-numbing, strawberry-flavoured candy. He could think of nothing else but those times when he'd watched the vet shove medication down cats' throats, and he tried to tell himself that this was similar. Sil needed the medication despite its attempts to dodge it, just like how some animals tried to dodge necessary shots at the vet. "Please, please forgive me ... " He took a deep breath, putting on his most authoritative face.

He walked back to the living room, sitting on the couch and prompting Sil to sit up. It wanted to hide more than anything, but Rayan willed himself to gently but firmly guide it into a sitting position.

"No medication," it sobbed, shaking its head, still trying to get away. "Please, sir, Rayan, please, *please*, you said you care, you said you *care*!"

Oh, Rayan's heart was shattering into a million pieces at the sight. He was doing it to save Sil. He was. He didn't want to hurt it, he *wasn't* hurting it, he wasn't giving it any pills that caused amnesia, he just had to get its fever down. "Sil, I'm sorry, I need you to take these. Please. They'll make you feel better."

That seemed to make the hysteria worse. The phrase set off something absolutely primal in the poor pet, and it put every ounce of its remaining strength and voice into protesting. It was getting way too loud for a little apartment with neighbours on all sides, and Rayan was getting anxious about being busted. In a panic, he decided that if physically forcing it was a no-go ... then he'd just bluff.

"If you don't take the medication here, I'll call the Agency and you can take it there."

Sil went rigidly still within a split second. Its eyes were impossibly wide, full of that animalistic fear Rayan had only ever seen once or twice in particularly bad cases of stray cats and dogs. That, and unbearable betrayal.

It took the pills without resistance, one after the other. Rayan eased it back down onto the sofa afterwards, trying not to think about the long-term effects this stupid trick would have on their relationship.

"I'm so sorry," he whispered miserably. His facade of having it all figured out and under control was long gone, and he slid down onto his knees next to the couch so as not to take up space that Sil might've needed. "Sil, I'm sorry, I had to say something – I had to get you to take those, I'm *so* sorry. I won't call them, okay? I was serious when I said I care, I swear. I – I just – " His desperate excuses came to a sudden stop when Sil closed its eyes, clearly indicating that it just wanted to rest and be left alone. Rayan swallowed and nodded to himself, a silent acknowledgment that he had fucked up. Of course, he had known that the moment he'd decided to force the medication.

He nervously ran his fingers through his hair. He needed help. He needed so much help. But from whom? He didn't want to get his family involved and get them into trouble, plus his parents would've skinned him alive for breaking the law like this. He couldn't ask a doctor – or could he?

He'd heard of ... underground vets before. He'd always thought the entire concept was repulsive. Pets and strays alike were supposed to go to actual vets, ones that were safe and monitored. Rich people also shouldn't have been encouraged to go outside of the system that had been set up to be as protective of registered pets as possible. But now that he had a stray on his hands, one he didn't want discovered ... maybe he could try to find something. Maybe ... god, he hated himself for thinking this way, but maybe he would even be able to bring Sil while it was sick and compliant enough. The fragile, barely-there trust they'd built had already been broken at this point; there was little to lose, and everything to gain.

"I ... I'm gonna be ... right here. In the, um ... in the kitchen. If you need anything ... " he trailed off when he got no response, getting up with a dejected sigh. He was just trying to keep it alive. Why was that so hard to do? Why did every decision that benefitted Sil physically seem like the worst possible option when it came to building some sort of emotional connection?

Rayan dragged himself back over to the kitchen, sitting down at the table and laying his head on his arms. He was an absolute monster for using the PPA as a threat, a thought only further confirmed when he heard the quiet sobbing from the living room. But what else was he supposed to do? He groaned, rubbing his face against his skin. Gross. He was so gross.

He had no idea how long he'd spent wallowing in self-pity before he heard a knock at the door. He jumped at the noise, his head snapping in the direction of his new pet. *Fuck*. He had to get Sil into the bedroom *immediately*.

"One moment!" he yelled, having to disregard the poor guy's consent *once again* as he hastily scooped it up along with its collar and brought it into the bedroom, setting it down on the bed. Thankfully, it seemed he'd woken it from a deep sleep, which meant it didn't even make a peep before the bedroom door was closed. He shoved the half-dried clothes into one of the cupboards, hoping he wouldn't forget to take them out afterwards. "Who is it?" he asked as he walked over, hand already on the doorknob.

"Pet Protection Agency," came the casual reply, and Rayan's blood froze in his veins.

Oh *god*.

Out of the Ordinary

Rayan stared at the door for a moment longer than he should've, only opening it when he was sure he wouldn't immediately throw up from the nerves. The sight of a young female agent greeted him, one that seemed incredibly exhausted and in general very much over the concept of having to talk to him.

"Rayan Kamali? I'm very sorry to bother you, sir," she began with a sigh, clicking her pen against her clipboard. "We've gotten a report about a stray from someone in the area, and we're obligated to ask around a bit. It will really only take a few minutes."

"Yeah – yeah, of course. Should we – would you like to come in?" he offered instinctively, almost flinching when he thought about the possibility of her discovering Sil. Lady Luck smiled upon him that day, because she declined, telling him again that it'd be quick.

The questions were simple enough: Have you seen a stray around? Have you seen anything out of the ordinary? Have you seen anyone stumbling about, looking lost or confused? They were textbook questions, taken straight from the PPA's official website, from the tab about recognising potential strays. It was difficult, given the striking resemblance they bore to people, so it was no wonder that any employee would be a little sceptical or frustrated about having to investigate a tenth false report.

Except this one was not fake.

Rayan answered everything to the best of his ability. He wasn't a very good liar, not even an average one. His palms were all sweaty, his voice broke, the lump in his throat refused to move either up or down. He kept chuckling nervously, repeating that he hadn't seen or heard anything multiple times. Most likely the only thing that saved him from incriminating himself completely was that she didn't let him ramble on, nor did she have the energy to be too suspicious.

"All done," she said after what had felt like an eternity to Rayan's battered heart. "Are you okay, sir?"

"Yeah!" he replied way too quickly. "Yeah, sorry. I get nervous about any questioning. It's like when I exit a store and I know I haven't stolen anything, but I'm like, *'oh god, what if it'll beep?'* That – that kinda thing. Sorry."

She gave him a sympathetic smile, the wariness disappearing from her face. "I'm really sorry if I've made you anxious. It's just a routine check. But please, if you see anything, don't hesitate to give us a call. It's likely nothing, though."

"Of course. I wouldn't want some poor guy to be stuck out there in the cold."

She nodded and went to knock on his neighbour's door, and Rayan forced himself to be slow about closing the door instead of slamming it shut. He took a few steps back, still holding his breath, only exhaling when he was far enough away that he thought she wouldn't hear.

Fucking hell. *Fucking hell.*

He wiped his hands off on his pants, but he couldn't stop the shaking. He'd just lied to a pet protection agent. If this got out, he would be fined *at the very least*. Could he go to jail for this? Misleading authorities? Probably yes. God, he didn't want to go to jail. His life was on track for once, his apartment was fairly clean, it looked like he was about to get promoted at work, he was steadily saving up money for that stupid dessert shop he wanted to open ... He couldn't go to jail.

Tears of pure, overwhelming stress were gathering in his eyes and quickly spilling over. He sat down on the floor, pulling his knees up to his chest, trying to calm himself. He needed to check on Sil and tell it that the coast was clear, the employee had left, and it wasn't going to be brought in. That was the obvious course of action in this situation, not weeping on the floor like a toddler. If he wanted to be a baby about it, he shouldn't have decided to do something so utterly illegal.

Wiping his eyes and taking one last, deep breath, Rayan stood up to go to the bedroom. He could hear the sound of footsteps going from the door to the bed as he approached, and he gave Sil a few moments to properly get into bed and pretend it hadn't been eavesdropping before knocking. "Sil?" No response. "Can I come in?"

It was a little silly. The bedroom was his own; Sil had barely been occupying it for more than ten minutes. Still, he had been so horribly evil, disregarding its consent and opinion at every turn, he felt obligated to at least give it this. Thus, he waited patiently, wondering whether Sil was pretending to be asleep.

Just when he was about to knock again, he heard a faint voice from inside. "No."

Admittedly, he was a little surprised. That wasn't the usual answer most people expected to a simple question like that. It wasn't even a question, really, not in any other scenario; it was more common courtesy, something nice but ultimately useless to say before entering a room. After having violated its consent multiple times, however, Rayan found it impossible to even touch the handle of the door.

"Okay," he said gently. "I just wanted to tell you that it's safe now."

Again, he waited for a good while for a response that truly didn't come this time. He didn't really know how to proceed. Sil had to come out eventually. Would he get his bedroom back then? No, Sil was better off inside, in a room that was hidden from people standing in the front doorway. But he still needed to get his bedsheets, even if he was going to sleep on the couch.

Well, the evening was still a long way away. "I'll come back later with some lunch, okay? Try to get some rest until then. I'm sorry everything is so stressful."

You made it stressful, a nasty voice in the back of his mind whispered. He tried to silence it, to no avail. He eventually decided to busy himself by opening up his laptop and doing some absolutely-not-suspicious research on underground vets. Opening a new tab in incognito mode seemed ridiculous, since he would be up against the government if he got caught, but he did it anyway, hoping to ease his anxiety a little.

There wasn't a lot of available information, of course. Not on sites that could be easily accessed by the masses. Most sources seemed to agree that to get into a clinic like that, one had to have two things: money and connections. As it stood, Rayan had neither.

He tilted his head back, letting it rest against the back of the couch. Connections ... Didn't he have anyone who could hook him up with a vet like that? Who would even have connections like that? People who wanted bad things to happen to pets, or people who wanted the opposite? Definitely people who had a reason to want to go around the system. People who didn't like the system.

Maybe ... people who thought the system was a scam and pets shouldn't have been treated like animals.

He typed in the name of the organisation as fast as he could, scrolling down to the bottom of their website to see their address. They weren't very far from where he lived, ironically, even though their beliefs couldn't have been further apart. He could barely believe he was about to throw himself at their feet.

The Pet Liberation organisation wasn't a very good one. Rayan saw the news about them, all those ludicrous things they kept spewing, trying to confuse people and turn them against the PPA. But even though they were a borderline cult, and Rayan agreed with virtually none of their sentiments, he had to admit that they definitely had a reason to visit or even operate underground pet clinics. But then again, could those clinics be trusted? Or would they employ actual doctors, ones specialised in caring for people?

It was a gamble either way, he supposed. It was a *huge* gamble, a leap of faith that had the potential to kill him. So many things could go wrong, he couldn't even count. What if they turned him away? What if they assumed he was some secret government official, trying to gather information? What if they reported him? What if the doctor they suggested was a complete whacko?

He put down the laptop and got up to pace around the living room. He had to get Sil to a vet one way or another, and this was the only thing he could think of. The only other option was to go to the PPA and let them handle it, but that one was basically out of the picture from the get-go. He just had to do some more research into the organisation's philosophy and pretend he was on board with them, right? Surely, they'd take pity on him if they knew how desperate the situation was. And it had to appeal to them as well, given that he was evading authorities to keep a pet safe. Sil already said he treated it too much like a person.

Or should he go immediately? He glanced at the bedroom door. He had no idea whether time was precious. Would the cold worsen? Was it more than a cold? Was it something serious? Would Sil even be okay in his apartment completely alone? Pets weren't made for independence, they needed someone to help them. But maybe if he just made it a quick errand –

A quiet little sneeze made him stop in his tracks. He could just imagine the poor thing shivering under the blanket. Maybe he should bring it one more layer, just to be safe, just to ensure it really wouldn't be cold anymore.

He grabbed his thickest quilt and made his way over to the bedroom before realising Sil had told him not to enter. He knocked again, deciding that if he wanted to talk to Sil about leaving it alone for a bit, he might as well ask whether he could bring the extra protection inside. "Hey, love? Would you like another blanket?"

"No," it rasped. "Just wanna be left alone."

Well, that's lucky. "Um, that's actually something I wanted to ask you – would it be okay if I left for a little bit? Will you be okay?"

No immediate answer. Rayan never knew what that meant. Was it just annoyed with him? Was it thinking about it? If so, what was the reason for the internal debate? Was it not sure it would be okay, or was it just trying to figure out where Rayan would go?

He could hear the creak of the bed and the shuffling of feet before the door was slowly opened. Sil stood there with the blanket around its shoulders, shaking with either the effort or cold. It had always seemed so small, but now that they were face to face with each other, Rayan could see that the pet was almost as tall as him. It looked ... scared, despite it trying to hide it. "Are you going to the shelter?" it asked quietly. "You can come inside. It's your room. I just ... I wanted to test it, I'm sorry. I won't be a bother." It shifted its weight from one foot to the other, losing its balance and almost fainting. Rayan caught its frail body at the last second, dropping the quilt to the floor. "Please don't call them," it muttered.

"Oh my god," he breathed, astounded by just how ... light and delicate it felt in his arms. It felt like a porcelain doll, about to shatter with the slightest pressure. He quickly brought it back to bed, laying it on the soft mattress and covering its body with the blanket. "I won't call the shelter, Sil. I'm sorry. I – I never meant to make you feel like you couldn't say no to me. I'm *so* sorry about the whole meds situation, I swear I just want to help you. I want you to get better, so you'll have the energy to tell me off like before, yeah?" He couldn't help getting a little choked up at the end, and he had to blink away some tears before he could go on. "I ... I need to get you help. I'm trying to get you help. But I'm not going to any shelter."

"Master ... Master would help ... "

Rayan had some doubts about that. "Can you tell me your master's name?"

Sil shook its head, burying its face in its hands after. It was sobbing again, and Rayan was starting to get very conscious about the possibility of dehydration.

"Hey, it's okay. Um ... if you really want to go back to your owner, then why ... why don't you want me to go to the shelter? They could read your chip there."

"No! No, no owner, no ... "

Rayan furrowed his brows in confusion. Okay, Sil was just talking nonsense. Was it delirious? This whole illness was most likely way worse than he'd thought. He needed to go and get a vet's appointment right now. "Okay, no owner. I'm gonna go and try to get you help, then, yeah? All according to the original plan. No shelter, no owner, just a doctor who can help cure you without blowing your cover. Sound good?"

"Doctor?" Its head lolled to the side, eyes fluttering closed. "Doctors would fix me ... But mutts don't deserve doctors ... "

"Mutts ... what?" It was so difficult to even listen to the things it said sometimes, Rayan couldn't even imagine actually living it. "Sil ... " He sighed heavily, wiping the fresh tears from his eyes. "You'll get better. I promise. I'll take you to a doctor, and they'll fix you up, and it'll all be alright."

Sil hummed approvingly. It took a lot of strength for Rayan to actually stand up and leave it lying there alone, but he wanted to get the contact info he needed as soon as possible. Who knew how long they'd have to wait to get an appointment? Were underground vets busy? They had to be.

He put the quilt over Sil, then brought it fresh water from the kitchen. He couldn't resist petting its hair a little when he checked whether its fever was going down, which, thankfully, felt like it was. "I'll lock the door so no one can bother you," he whispered. "I'll be back before you know it."

Pet Liberation

There was little that Rayan hated more than the Pet Liberation movement. Cult, even, if the media was anything to go by. He didn't necessarily like to jump on any hate trains, but the one against this specific movement seemed to be more than justified. Everything they did, everything they believed in ... It was all nonsense, and they were very angry and violent about it.

Science had long proven that pets were different. Not in a bad way, but in a way that cats were different from dogs. They needed different care, different accommodations ... Their entire brain chemistry was different, their habits, their behaviours, it was all so different from the way people were. Pets were just different. And yet, Pet Lib continued to spew the nonsense that pets and people were one and the same, and the only thing separating them from each other were drugs and conditioning. Hell, they said that any one person could be taken from the street and turned into a pet within a matter of months. They said that was the exact scenario some strays found themselves in.

Rayan tried not to think about all this. He was going to their central office to talk to some very important people; he couldn't rile himself up with the lies right before that. But still, he couldn't *not* think about it. What was wrong with these people? Yes, some strays had lived a substantial portion of their lives thinking they were people. But they could feel that something was wrong! That was why there was an entire process for strays turning themselves over! It caused severe distress in them to be living as people! To call that kidnapping and human trafficking – god, he couldn't imagine what was going through the minds of some people.

He looked down at his hands, fidgeting anxiously. He was going to entrust some seriously sensitive information to these people. If they said something outrageous, like, "Well, let Sil go, let it live as a person!" he didn't know what he was going to say. Should he play along? It'd likely frighten the poor pet if later the vet told it some similar things.

Well, he would think about crossing that bridge when it was at the very least in sight. He got off the bus at the next stop, walking over to the small office building on the other side of the street. This was it, then. He was about to talk to some very strange people.

"Good morning, sir, how may I help you?" a kind woman behind the desk asked, and Rayan suddenly realised he had no idea how to reach the people he wanted to reach.

"I ... um ... I was wondering if I could talk to ... someone. Like, someone who knows a lot about this whole conspiracy." Yes, that was good. He'd seen the word conspiracy used on their website several times in relation to the pet system. "I'm very sorry, I haven't been a follower of the movement for a very long time, but ... it abruptly became ... quite personal to me. To, um, learn about this."

"I'm very sorry to hear that, sir," she said gently. "Understanding the system that causes our grief and working to change it can give our life purpose, I think. I'll try to see if I can reach one of our educators, or you could take a pamphlet in the meantime. We hold weekly meetings and demonstrations, completely free of charge, if you're interested."

"Thank you so much. I'll wait here, then." He took a pamphlet from the desk and sat down, skimming the text.

The faux-science of the Pet Protection Agency. Facts or well-marketed propaganda?

'Strays' are not being saved – the realities of the 'pet test'.

The culture that raised us to let our loved ones be kidnapped and thank the kidnappers.

Corruption, custom pets, and the abuse behind closed doors.

The purposely shocking titles brought back all his memories of the research he'd done, and he felt like he was going to be sick. He quickly stuffed the paper in his pocket, taking a couple deep breaths to calm himself. These people were *evil*. How could they actually spread things like this? How could they go out there and yell all these things at the top of their lungs, as if – as if they were *true*?

They were preying on vulnerable people: ones who had lost a loved one due to them being discovered to have been a pet, ones who had relatives go to jail for pet abuse, strays ... They really were a cult. They had recruited all these ignorant and desperate people who weren't in the right state of mind to join any movement and told them to recruit more. But all that senseless spouting of nonsense could only ever lead to two outcomes, one of which was the complete loss of that friendship, and the other was a successful recruitment. Which meant that these people had ended up with no one but their own cult around them, trapped in the echo chamber of a harmful ideology.

"Sir?"

Rayan's head snapped towards the receptionist woman, then he quickly stood up to go back to the desk.

"One of our educators is available. If it's alright for you, she could be here within ten minutes to answer all your questions." She covered the microphone of the phone, lowering her voice. "I told her that it seemed urgent. I hope that's okay."

"Yes, thank you. Thank you *so* much. I can wait here – or if it's better for her someplace else, I can go there – I can pay her for her time too, I know this was really sudden, and I've never donated to the movement – "

The woman smiled and put a finger up, silencing him. She quickly ended the phone call, then turned back to Rayan with such genuine compassion in her eyes that it pained him to even return her gaze. He was lying to these people. These poor, misguided people who just wanted to do good in the world in their own way. "Denice won't accept a single coin from you, most likely. It's deeply personal for a lot of us, but she's someone who has lost *a lot* to this cruelty. She'll be able to answer any questions you might have."

Rayan nodded wordlessly. He let the woman rant about the injustices in this world, about the fact that she would've moved to Batum long ago if she didn't think they had a chance to change things here. Those people knew what they were doing. They had outlawed the keeping of pets ages ago. They treated everyone as equals.

He wished these people would understand that *people* were treated equally in Lezune. But pets weren't people, that was the whole point, the whole reason behind treating them differently. Treating different beings similarly was just as much of an injustice as treating similar beings differently. He had learned about the effects of the Batumian pet-ban in high school, same as everyone else. Same as the woman sitting across from him, probably. He knew damn well that it had caused serious issues within the country, ones they were still trying desperately to recover from. The pets they tried to integrate into their society of people weren't doing any better than if they had tried to integrate sheep into a wolf enclosure. It just didn't work like that.

When Denice arrived, she suggested they go into one of the more secluded rooms, so Rayan could talk openly. He readily agreed, stiffly settling into one of the comfortable armchairs in the little office she had led him to. He didn't know where to begin.

"I don't mean to assume anything," she started instead, with a knowing look that made Rayan feel like she could see right through him. "But I think you don't really care about the movement. In fact, I think you think we're out of our minds."

"That's – no, of course not – "

She smiled. "I'm not a mindreader or anything, please don't look so worried. I frequent the restaurant you work at, and I've heard you talk about your big dream to adopt a pet so many times I can't even count."

Oh. Rayan's face flushed with embarrassment, and he resolved to share less with his coworkers, or at least do so in a lower volume. He rubbed the back of his neck awkwardly, trying to think of a lie big enough that it would justify him changing his whole worldview. He couldn't.

"I didn't want to lie," he said quietly. "I'm sorry. I didn't know how else to get a hold of … someone. Anyone who could help."

"Well, I still want to. I didn't come to the office just to scold you and send you on your way. We're not out for people's blood, Rayan. I just didn't want to build this entire conversation on a lie."

He took a deep breath and nodded, meeting Denice's eyes again. "I found a stray. It's very sick right now, and it's also badly injured. I didn't report it to anyone, because I think its previous owner was the one who caused most of its injuries, and from what I gather, it has never been taken to a vet before."

"And you can't take it to a government-approved clinic, so you came here to ask if we had any clinics outside of the system," she concluded. He nodded again. Denice leaned back in her chair, humming in thought.

"You know I'm not a secret PPA officer or anything," Rayan tried weakly. "I mean, if you've seen me at work – you know they don't need to work as waiters and waitresses. Please. If you can direct me to anyone who could possibly help ... I don't want it to go back to a place where it's being hurt. I don't want it to suffer. Even – even if I don't agree with a lot of what you guys are saying, isn't that the whole point? To reduce suffering?"

"You're asking me to break the law, Rayan. You're asking me to give up information I may or may not have on an underground clinic that you could direct absolutely anyone to. You're not part of the movement, in fact you're *against* the movement, and yet you're asking me for sensitive information that could put several of us in jail."

He swallowed thickly, unable to argue. "Yeah. Yeah, that's ... I guess that's what I'm asking. But I'm also already breaking the law. If I contacted the authorities now, I would be in trouble too."

"I don't even know if you have actually found anyone."

"Should I take pictures? Voice recordings? What do you need me to do?" he asked desperately. "What do I need to do so you'll trust me? Please, it almost fainted when it tried to stand. It's alone in my apartment right now and I just want to go home and tend to it, but I *need* to get in contact with a vet. I don't think I can help it alone. I'm already trusting you with all the sensitive information you need to land me in jail, *please*, give me a chance. I'll join the movement if that's what you need."

"We're not that strapped for members." Denice stood up from her desk, motioning for Rayan to do the same. "I'll send someone to check out the situation. If they think you're fine, you'll get to go meet our doctor. Does that sound fair?"

"Why won't you come?" he blurted out, and she laughed.

"I can't visit randos anymore. If I go to anyone's house, the PPA will start harassing them too, thinking they're new recruits. If you're really hiding a 'stray' in there, it'll be discovered within days."

Rayan stood up and nodded. "Right. Sorry. Thank you so much for helping me. I really can't even explain how much it means. I'm so – I'm just so worried."

She put a gentle hand on his shoulder. "Don't take this as an insult, but I think we'll see each other a lot more in the future. You seem like a pretty good guy, and if you're going about this the illegal way, you'll very quickly realise that we might not be the cultists here."

He didn't have much time to react before she passed him on the way to the door, and he quickly followed after her. Before he knew it, he was already on the bus back home, hoping that the Pet Liberation secret agent they were going to send would find everything in order. At least enough to give him the doctor's contact info.

Assessment

On the way back, Rayan's head was full of doubts and concerns. Did he make a mistake? Would Denice report him? No, that'd mean implicating herself. Not to mention what she'd said about the PPA 'harassing' everyone she came into contact with.

On that same note, though, would Rayan be harassed? Would they mistakenly assume he aligned with Pet Lib?

Would they never give him a licence because of that?

He got off the bus a stop too late, but he decided to take it as a blessing in disguise. A little walk would do him good, it'd allow him to clear his head.

No, he couldn't dilly-dally. He picked up his pace, pushing past the people lazily strolling along. He had someone waiting now. Someone very sick.

He made a quick stop at the pharmacy to pick up some more cold medicine, hoping that next time he wouldn't have to resort to cheap bluffs that made Sil's heart skip several beats. He hoped Sil would be better by the time he got home, but he didn't want to get his hopes up. He didn't even worry about it escaping as of now, which was really just a testament to what condition he'd left it in.

"I'm home," he said softly as he finally entered his apartment. Nothing looked amiss, everything was exactly as he'd left it. There was no response from the bedroom, but that could've been for a number of reasons. Maybe Sil was just asleep – still, he would've been lying if he'd said his heart was beating normally.

He tiptoed over to the bedroom door and turned his head to the side, pressing his ear against the wood. There were no sounds coming from inside. He put a hand on the handle and tried to push it down as slowly as possible, just until he heard the telltale click of it popping open. He paused, listening for any sounds – nothing.

The door slid open soundlessly, and Rayan was met with one of the most terrifying sights he could've imagined: an empty bed, devoid of the stray he'd painstakingly carried home with him.

"Fuck!" He pushed the door all the way open, rushing over to the bed in a frenzy. The mattress was still warm in the middle, just where he'd laid Sil, so it must've left not too long ago. Maybe if he ran –

Achoo.

Rayan froze in place. Did someone just ... sneeze? It came from the direction of the bed. From ... under the bed.

He slowly lowered himself to the ground, getting on his hands and knees and bending down until he could see under the bed. There it was, staring back at him with puffy, red eyes. "Sil ... "

Achoo.

No wonder it was sneezing so much, he hadn't cleaned under the bed in ages.

"I wasn't sure it was you," it mumbled, eyes already half-closing. It must've taken so much effort to squeeze under the bed like that, especially in its state. "I didn't want ... others to see ... " Was it dozing off mid-sentence?

Rayan sighed. "It's okay. It's just me. Come on, out we go."

He pulled out his pet without much resistance from it, gently laying it on the bed again. He meticulously removed every last dust bunny that had gotten stuck to its pyjamas before covering it with several blankets again, unable to resist some encouraging words as he worked. Sil didn't seem to mind. In fact, the murmurs seemed to help it relax.

"I went and talked to a kind lady by the name of Denice," he said quietly. "She said she'll send a friend to assess your situation. They're not connected to the PPA in any way; in fact, the PPA kind of hates them. Those are the only type of people I can really talk to right now, I suppose."

"Assess ... ?"

"They'll take a look at you. See how sick you are. Then, if they can help, they'll connect us with a nice doctor. Someone who won't hurt you or turn you in."

"A doctor ... " Sil rubbed its face against the pillow. "I'd like a doctor ... "

"Yeah, I'd like one too. I'm not very good at medical stuff." Rayan slowly reached out, letting the back of his hand brush against Sil's forehead. The fever seemed to be going down at least. He experimentally petted it a little, gently ruffling its hair; Sil leaned into it. "Did you climb under the bed when you heard me enter?"

"Mhm."

"I'll clean out the closet for you, how about that? You can have your little hiding place in there. I'll also clean out the entire room so you don't have to crawl around in filth. I'm so sorry for not having done it sooner, I just had no idea you'd do this ... I don't know why, I should've known you'd get scared ... "

"Rayan?"

"Yes?"

"Can you bring me ... the clothes? My clothes?"

"They're drying on the radiator in the living room." Shit, that was a lie. He totally forgot he'd thrown them into the cupboard. Thank god Sil mentioned it. "I mean, um ... I can bring them inside, put them on the radiator here. If that's okay. I don't want you cuddling wet clothes, they'll just make you sicker."

"Radiator's fine," it mumbled. Its eyes were already closing again, and Rayan wagered it would be asleep by the time he got back from the other room.

"You can go back to sleep, love," he said gently. "I'll place them on the radiator and close the bedroom door again. I won't wake you for the visit if I don't have to."

"I wanna be awake ... Wanna see ... I wanna see the doctor ... "

"This won't be the doctor yet. Just a friend who might tell us about the doctor. Just sleep, sweetheart. Don't even worry about it."

"Mhm ... "

***

The next time someone knocked on the door, Rayan was quick to open it without so much as a question. "I'm so glad you were able to make it," he said to the strange man standing on his doorstep. He didn't ... look like a secret agent.

"Of course, Rayan, anything for my dear friend!" he said cheerily. Great, he already knew his name, while Rayan knew absolutely nothing. "Let's see what we're working with – "

"Can you keep it down a little?" he asked once the door was closed. "It's sleeping."

"Oh, yes, yes, of course." He made a zipping motion from one corner of his mouth to the other. "Not a sound from me. Are they in the bedroom?"

"Yeah, I had to bring it in there because – "

"Ah! None of that dehumanising language until I hear it from their own mouth that they want that. No referring to people as 'it' without their express permission. Or as 'pets', while we're at it."

"Its – their throat hurts. Don't make it – them speak, if you can help it. Please. They're really sick."

The man nodded. "Lead the way, then."

Rayan walked past him and pushed the bedroom door open, revealing a very much asleep Sil. The man peeked inside, then gave Rayan an apologetic look. "I'll have to wake them."

"Well ... I mean, if it can't be helped ... " Rayan sighed. "I'll go wake it instead. Just – just give me a moment." He walked over and sat on the bed, and Sil's eyes already fluttered open. "Hey, sweet. Our friend has arrived, yeah? He'll take a quick look at you now. Are you alright with that?"

The man gave a slightly awkward wave. "Hi. I'm the friend."

Sil glanced at him before its gaze returned to Rayan. "Who's that?"

"Well, um ... I'm sorry, I didn't even ask your name – "

"Not important," the man said quickly. "Let's just get this over with, and I'll be out of here in a second."

The stranger produced an odd-looking device from his coat pocket, the likes of which Rayan had never seen before. He held it up to Sil's neck until it beeped, then stepped back. "Chipped. Poor thing."

Right. All pets were chipped. If this man got it to a doctor, they could simply read its chip, and then the mystery of who its owner was would immediately be solved –

"Can you tell me your name?"

Rayan was pulled back to the present moment as the man started his questioning. He looked at Sil, who looked like it took it a considerable effort to answer. "Dunno."

"You don't know what your name is?"

"Don't have one."

Rayan almost wanted to chime in, but felt like it'd be rude. If Sil didn't want to give its name to this person, he could understand it.

"Alright. Do you have a number?"

Sil frowned. "No. Owner said I didn't deserve one."

Oh, how that pained Rayan to hear. Was Sil's owner someone wealthy? Someone wealthy enough to keep multiple pets and only numbered them instead of naming them? He'd heard of such cases, but didn't realise someone in the area would be like that.

"Did you have a number before your owner?"

"Dunno."

"Alright. Are you a pet?"

"Yes."

"Would you like to be referred to as 'it'?"

"Yes."

Rayan resisted the urge to say 'I told you so'.

"Rayan, I'm going to have to ask you to step outside for a moment."

"What?" Rayan looked at Sil, then back at the man. "Why? What did I do?"

"I want him to stay," Sil said suddenly, and Rayan had never felt more proud in his life.

"It wants me to stay," he echoed.

"It'll just be a moment," he assured them.

"I want him to stay," Sil repeated, more firmly this time. It seemed to be getting really agitated over the idea of having to stay alone with a stranger.

"Okay, fine. I'll just ask in front of him. Is there anything you want me to know about? Did Rayan hurt you at all? Is he the reason you're so sick?"

Rayan's heart dropped. Technically ... yes. Yes, he was the reason why Sil was so sick now. But he hadn't hurt it. Would Sil say otherwise? Would it bring up the way he'd tricked it into taking medication? The way he'd failed to invite it into his warm home until it was halfway frozen?

The man seemed to take notice of his nerves, and Rayan averted his gaze. If Sil said something, he'd deserve it. It might even get Sil taken from him, but maybe then it'd be in the hands of more qualified people.

But then again, it had asked for him to stay. Surely, if Sil harboured any resentment towards him, it would be happy to be rid of him. Or maybe it was just a 'devil you know' scenario for it. Rayan had no way of telling.

"No," Sil said simply, and Rayan couldn't hold back a relieved sigh. "He helped me."

"Understood," the man said with a nod. "Rayan, if you'd be so kind … "

"Yes, of course. I'm coming." He jumped up from the bed to escort him out, anxiously awaiting the verdict.

"It's most definitely a 'pet'," he started once they were out of the bedroom, doing air-quotes with his hands, "and a very worn-down one at that. It's been a while since I've seen something so severe. I'll write down the contact of the doctor; call her between six and eight in the evening. Don't forget about the chip in its neck, that could get very dangerous for both of you. Get it treated."

Before he knew it, Rayan was standing in his almost empty apartment with a little note in his hand.

He did it. He passed. He now had the contact information of an underground vet.

DOCTOR'S APPOINTMENT

Time seemed to slow down as Rayan waited for the clock to strike six. He was sitting on the couch, staring at the one he'd gotten as a housewarming gift from his sister, Dana, bouncing his leg in anxiety as he tried to go through what he was going to say in his head.

"Hi, my name is Rayan. A Pet Lib guy gave me your number and I'd like to schedule an appointment for as soon as possible."

The less details, the better. Right? He could explain everything in greater detail once he and Sil were there. Or she'd see for herself, really. Honestly, Rayan didn't quite know the extent of Sil's injuries, nor how it'd sustained them. The only thing he knew about was it catching this nasty cold, for which he was going to assume full responsibility.

He jumped when his phone's reminder went off. Six o'clock. It was time.

He quickly dialled the number he'd been given, waiting nervously as the phone rang. "Hello?"

"Um, hi." He gripped the phone a little tighter, trying to swallow the lump in his throat. The woman on the other side sounded kind – honestly, everyone associated with Pet Lib had been kind so far – but he still couldn't shake the feeling that this was *wrong*. "My name is Rayan, and I've been given your number by a Pet Lib guy. I don't know his name, I'm sorry. Um, I was just wondering, uh ... if you could give me an appointment? As soon as possible, please."

"I'll give you the address, and you can tell me how soon you can get there. Does that sound alright?"

"Wait, like, today? Right now?"

"You said as soon as possible. I take my job seriously, Rayan."

"Right, right, sorry."

"My office is about five minutes from the address I'm about to tell you. I can't tell you the exact address for safety reasons, but I'll be there to help."

Rayan listened intently as she recited the address, immediately looking it up on his laptop to see where it was. "I can get there in half an hour. Is that alright?"

"That's fine. I'll be there to pick you up in exactly half an hour. What car do you drive?"

None, as of now. But he couldn't say that. He wouldn't be able to carry Sil through the city in the state it was in, so he'd need to ask his sisters for their car. "I don't really know the model, um, it's red. I'll give you the licence plate number, if that's okay."

Once arrangements were made, Rayan hung up and let out a relieved sigh. Everything was going to be fine, he told himself. He hoped his sisters didn't need the car for the rest of the evening.

***

"How much longer?" Sil asked miserably from the backseat. It was lying down with a blanket to cover it, but its shivering was still more than noticeable. "'m really cold … "

"Two minutes, love. Just hold on a little longer, and the doctor will help you. I promise."

Suddenly, there was a knock on the window. Both Rayan and Sil jumped, and the pet immediately ducked under the covers. Whoever was trying to get Rayan's attention didn't look like the kind elderly lady he'd imagined while talking on the phone – in fact, he didn't look like any lady at all.

He quickly rolled down the window. "Can I help you?"

"You can't park here," he said gruffly.

"I – w   hat? Why? I didn't see a sign – "

"I'm telling you that you can't."

Rayan blinked a couple times, confused. If he was made to park somewhere else, there was no telling whether the doctor would find him. "But I have to. I have – I'm meeting someone."

The man raised an eyebrow. "And who might you be meeting *here*?"

"I'm sorry, I don't think that's – "

"Milo, stop bothering the customer."

That sounded more like the voice from the phone call. Rayan craned his neck to look past the buff man by his window, and he spotted a short lady briskly walking towards his car.

The man – Milo – huffed. "I've never seen him around before. He doesn't look the type."

"Well, I'm telling you that he is. Stand down, boy."

Was Milo a pet? In his words, he didn't … look the type. In fact, he looked like the scariest person Rayan had ever had the displeasure of meeting.

But he did stand down, allowing the doctor to walk up to his car window. "Rayan, am I correct?"

"Yes, ma'am. Can we go to the office now?" Maybe he was glancing at Milo way too noticeably, but the doctor let out a little laugh.

"Yes. Don't worry about Milo; he can be a little overbearing, but his heart is in the right place. And he'd never hurt a fly. My name is Anne, by the way." She stepped back so Rayan could open the door. "Do we need a stretcher for the little guy?"

"No, I can bring it in. Just give me a moment."

Rayan had never been to this part of the city. He couldn't help looking around every two seconds, anxious that someone other than Milo could be following them. The buildings looked old and quite unstable, most of the street lamps didn't work, and rubbish was thrown on the sidewalk in piles. He was honestly a little hesitant when it came to bringing Sil into an office, afraid that it might be in similar conditions.

He couldn't have been more wrong.

The office was as sterile as any other doctor's office he'd seen, if only a little small and not that well-equipped. He laid Sil on the examination table and stepped back, surprised to see it reach out for him.

"Don't leave," it croaked out, and Rayan stepped closer to hold its hand.

"I'm not leaving, love. I'm just trying to give the doctor space to work. I promise, I'm not leaving."

"Quite attached, are we?" Dr. Anne asked as she put on some gloves. "That's good. I would've been really angry if it turned out you were a *bad* illegal owner."

"I love pets," Rayan said defensively. "And I love Sil. I want it to be okay, that's the whole reason I'm here."

"Oh, don't get all mad at me. When you've been an illegal doctor for long enough, you learn not to get your hopes up every time. Many of my clients are the rich fucks who want to avoid scrutiny after beating their pet senseless."

Rayan felt his guts churn, and even Sil whimpered. "And you help them?" it asked in a small voice.

"I do what I do for the pets. What sense is there in turning those people away? The pet would suffer the consequences."

She stepped up to the table. "And if I didn't help them, their owners might bring them to worse doctors. I've seen some truly gnarly injuries in my time – I don't trust the other underground clinics. Now, let's see what the problem is with you."

Rayan was trying very hard to sit still as Dr. Anne examined Sil, but it was proving to be quite difficult. She seemed to be causing quite a lot of discomfort, especially when she began moving the badly healed limbs around.

"We'll have to rebreak these if we want them to heal well," she said after a while. "I don't know exactly what happened, but I assume you didn't get medical attention for it."

"Rebreak?" Sil asked, eyes widening in horror. "No! No, please! Don't touch me! Don't hurt me!"

Rayan jumped up from his chair immediately. "Hey, Sil, calm down. Calm down, it's okay. It wouldn't be like the first time at all. It'd be nothing like that." Dr. Anne stepped back so he could take her place and take Sil by the hand, rubbing soothing circles into its skin. "You'd be asleep for it. Right, doctor?"

"Of course," she said without missing a beat. "We're not barbarians here."

"I don't want my limbs broken!" it cried anyway. "We need to go! I want to go home! Leave me alone! Master will be so mad that you broke my limbs again, Master will be furious! Master will save me!"

"Oh, sweetheart … " Rayan moved on to petting its hair instead, trying to stay calm in the face of it lashing out. "It's okay.

We just want to help. If you agree to the procedure, Dr. Anne will be able to make the pain go away. You're in a lot of pain, aren't you? You can barely walk."

"And if I don't agree? Then you'll report me?"

"No, no, of course not. Sil, I'm sorry about that." Dr. Anne shot him a suspicious glance, and Rayan felt his cheeks heat up. "I ... I tried to get it to take the cold medicine, but it didn't want to, so ... so I said ... I said I'd send it to the PPA so they could take care of it ... I realise that was horrible of me. I just wanted its fever to break, I swear. I was so scared."

She let out a heavy sigh. "Right. Well, there will be no more threats like that after this point. Unless Sil consents to the procedure, I'm not touching it."

"But you have to! It can barely walk – "

Dr. Anne glared at him. "Rayan, let me tell you something. The day I start doing non-consensual surgeries on people is the day I'll just apply to work at the PPA instead."

Rayan shut his mouth and slowly nodded. Right. He was being quite a horrible person, wasn't he? Dr. Anne was absolutely right. "I'm sorry," he said quietly.

"I don't want my bones broken," Sil muttered.

"Then they won't be. But let me give you a rundown on how that procedure would go – if you decide against it afterwards, I'll just send you on your way with some medicine for that nasty cold you got."

Rayan sat back in his chair, zoning out a little while the explanation was happening. He was much too preoccupied with his internal dilemma to pay much attention.

Was the PPA right to deny him a licence for pet ownership? Was there something wrong with him? But pets had to be treated without their consent sometimes, right? Like dogs, cats, or even children. Some just can't consent to surgeries that would objectively be good for them. There were no consent forms for pets. Was he wrong to bring Sil to an underground vet? Or doctor. Or whatever Dr. Anne was, he wasn't even sure.

What if Sil wasn't going to consent? Would there be serious consequences? Rayan wouldn't have minded if it was a cosmetic procedure, or something entirely optional, but he'd seen how much pain Sil was in every time it had to move around. This didn't feel optional.

"Rayan?"

He looked up to see both Sil and the doctor staring at him. "I – I'm sorry, I wasn't listening. Yes?"

Sil bit its lower lip, suddenly hesitating. "Would … would you be here the whole time? During surgery?"

Rayan glanced at Dr. Anne, who gave him a small nod of approval. "Yes. Yes, of course. Anything you want."

It squirmed a little, eyes darting between him and the doctor. "And it wouldn't hurt?"

"Not at all. You'd be asleep for the whole thing, I promise," the doctor said soothingly.

Sil swallowed. "O-okay. I think ... Okay. If it really won't hurt ... But Rayan must stay. Please. Please, don't leave while I'm asleep. Not again."

Rayan furrowed his brows in confusion. "Again?"

"Master disappeared," it mumbled. "I fell asleep, and ... and then they were gone."

"I won't leave," he promised again, filing that information away in his mind for later. He wasn't going to pry in front of the doctor. "I'll be right here when you wake up. I promise."

Sil nodded. Dr. Anne moved on to sterilise her equipment.

This would be a long night.

MASTER

Taking Sil home after surgery was easier than taking it there. It was still mostly out of it from the anaesthetics, napping peacefully in the backseat of the car. Rayan tried not to jostle it as he took it inside, then rushed back to take the car to his sisters' apartment. Once everything was settled – and he'd told Dana and Nima some lie about where he'd been – he assumed his guardian position next to Sil's bed.

"Rayan ... " it moaned quietly, reaching for him as soon as he entered the room. "Hurts ... "

"That's okay. It's alright. The doctor has prescribed you a lot of pain medication, I'll just – "

"No ... No pills ... Not again ... "

Fuck. "Sil ... "

"I am not consenting ... " it slurred. "No consent ... No ... "

"Sil, they'll make the pain go away. I have to give you medication for it, otherwise you'll be in pain for *weeks* on end. The doctor gave you medicine too, and you were fine afterwards.

71

You didn't forget anything, did you? And I was right there when you woke up, just like I promised."

Sil's head lolled to the side, and it closed its eyes again. "No medicine … "

Rayan sighed and grabbed his chair, pulling it right up next to the bed. "Alright. No consent, no medicine. Dr. Anne chewed me out for that bluff enough, I'm not doing it again."

"You said the doctor would fix me … Why do I need more medicine … ?"

"Well … it gets worse before it gets better, a lot of the time. It will get worse for a bit – "

"Worse?" Sil looked up at him, its eyes full of horror. "Worse than how it was? But you said she'd fix me! You said … I wanna be better, I wanna be without pain … "

"You will be. If you don't trust me, trust Dr. Anne. She promised your limbs would go back to how they were. You'll just need a few weeks – "

"Weeks?" Sil let out a heavy sigh. "I don't wanna wait weeks … "

"You don't have to wait out those weeks in pain. That's what the medication is for. It won't make you forget anything, it'll just make your weeks bearable. Don't you want to give it a try?"

Sil shook its head frantically. "No medicine. No pills."

It was Rayan's turn to sigh. "Alright. No pills for now. But the offer is on the table for whenever you change your mind."

A horrible little thought weaseled its way into Rayan's mind as he watched his pet all out of it. Would it be easier to get information out of it now? If he were to ask about its master, would it clear up some of the confusion? If he asked about the collar or the tag, would it answer?

These were all horrible thoughts, but they were almost impossible to ignore. He needed answers if he were to help this poor pet. He needed to know where to return it, whether its master was really a horrible person ...

"Sil?"

"Mhm ... "

Rayan was fidgeting with the hem of his shirt, not even really looking at the pet as he spoke. "Was your master a good person?"

Silence. "Yes. I love my master."

"Did they ever hurt you?"

"No."

Rayan's heartbeat picked up. Did he make all the wrong assumptions? "How did you get all these injuries, then?"

Sil shivered, even under the blanket. It must've been the anxiety. "Owner hurt me."

Rayan frowned. "But you said – "

"Not Master. Master would never hurt me."

Slowly, painstakingly slowly, it was starting to dawn on Rayan; Sil was talking about two different people. Owner and Master were not just synonyms to it, they marked two very different personalities.

"Oh," he breathed. But that was strange. Pets with several owners over the years should've been wiped between rehomings. How did Sil remember its previous master? "What was Master like?"

"Kind ... Always so kind to me ... I can't remember very well ... I remember little things, like – like Master holding me, singing me to sleep ... I remember a lake, and – and sitting on the shore in the grass ... The sun reflected off the water so prettily, I loved sitting there ... "

A lake? There was no lake near Laka. The only water near Laka was maybe the river Vezi, but that most definitely wasn't a lake. "Don't you mean the river?" he tried.

"Lake ... It was a lake ... Master loved the lake, and I loved it too, and we'd sit on the shore, and they'd brush my hair, and it was all so calm ... "

A lake. Lake Havey, maybe? But that was hours away from Laka. Maybe this was the wrong line of questioning. "What was your owner like?"

Sil shivered again. "*Bad*. Bad, horrible, mean ... Everyone was mean ... Owner was mean, his sister was mean, the other pets were mean ... It always hurt, something always, *always* hurt, and they'd yell at me, and beat me ... "

Rayan's heart twisted in pain. "Sil, I'm so sorry."

"He broke my bones too. But he never let me be asleep. He'd break them while I was awake, and he'd never take me to the doctor, and he'd yell at me for being in pain ... "

The topic was clearly upsetting the poor pet, and Rayan decided to try to shift the conversation. "Do you remember his name, maybe? Even just a first name?"

Sil shook its head. "Never told me. I don't know. I just called him master, or sir."

"Were you still by the lake when this new owner took over?"

"I don't know. I was never allowed outside."

Rayan winced. That was absolutely horrible. "How did you escape, then?"

"Owner left my door open one day on accident. Or maybe on purpose ... I was in a lot of pain, so maybe he thought I wouldn't get up anyway ... But I did. I ran. I ran until I collapsed and couldn't anymore. I got on random buses that looked like they'd take me far away. But then my leg started to hurt a lot ... "

"How did you get on buses? I thought – "

"I stole money. I stole food. I stole whatever I could. I just wanted to get back to the lake. I wanted to find Master."

Rayan nodded solemnly. "I get that. I'm sorry about ... everything that happened to you. It's awful."

"Master will fix it. Owner said Master sold me, that Master didn't want me anymore, but I know it's not true. Master loved me, and I loved Master so much. I know they'll fix it, once I find them ... They'll fix it all ... I'll never be in pain anymore, once I'm back with Master ... "

"The collar you love so much, is it from your master?" Sil nodded. Rayan didn't bring up the tag he'd found in Sil's pocket. It seemed inappropriate, even during an already inappropriate questioning. "I see. Well ... you should probably go back to sleep now. I don't wanna bother you. I'll make my bed on the couch, and if you need anything, just call for me. Okay?"

Sil looked up at him with the saddest eyes he'd ever seen. "You won't stay?"

"I, well ... I assumed you wouldn't want me to," he admitted. "Should I just stay here? Sleep on a mattress on the floor? I'll be waking up early tomorrow to go to work. Won't I bother you?"

Sil shook its head. "I don't wanna be alone ... I'm scared ... "

Rayan couldn't say no to that. "Alright. I'll take out the spare mattress and sleep here with you. And again, if you need anything, don't hesitate to wake me up."

BUBBLES

The next day, Sil didn't remember having a conversation about its master. Rayan tried to allude to it, tried to gently prod and see just how much he could reveal ... but apparently none of it. Sil was oblivious.

This was bad.

"You don't remember talking about the collar either?"

Sil looked at him with big, innocent – albeit a bit suspicious – eyes. "My collar?"

"We ... we talked a bit about it."

Sil narrowed its eyes. "What did we talk about?"

Rayan squirmed on his mattress. "Well, um ... "

"I was barely there yesterday. I don't even remember anything. Just *what* did you ask me about in that state?"

"Sil ... "

"No, I want to know. I have a right to know. I don't have many rights – I barely have any at all. But I do know I have a right to know what you asked me about when I was half-asleep and barely conscious. Right out of surgery."

Rayan sighed. "I asked you about your owner. And your master. I ... I know they're two different people. And – " Was this the time to share the fact that he'd seen the tag?

"And ... ?" it prompted, leaning closer. "What else?"

"You ... um ... I mean, *I* ... " Rayan averted his gaze, shifting awkwardly. "When I first brought you inside, your clothes were sopping wet. I had to put them on the radiator. As I was doing that, something fell out of your pocket ... "

Sil's eyes went wide as two saucepans. Its good arm shot out to touch its pocket, the tag nestled safely inside from when Rayan had put it back. "You're disgusting!" it hissed. "You went through my things!"

"I didn't! It was an accident!" Rayan tried not to raise his voice, both to avoid scaring Sil and to avoid alerting the neighbours to its presence. "It was an accident, I swear! I – at that point, I couldn't just leave it ... I just wanted to see what it was, so I – "

"So you looked at it! You read it!"

"I'm sorry!"

Sil wanted to say more, but it turned into a coughing fit. Rayan had to resist the urge to rush over to rub its back – he assumed that wouldn't have been taken kindly. Instead, he just sat there, looking dumb and useless.

"Sil ... " he started gently once the coughing stopped. "I'm sorry. It was just right there – I just wanted to help. I wanted to know who your owner was so I could help you. I didn't even know back then – I didn't know you've gone through multiple of them."

"What did it say?" Sil asked.

"Huh?"

"What did my tag say?" it asked again, more urgent.

"I ... You don't know?"

Sil shook its head. "I ... I can't read. I can sometimes read – if something's written out in large, clear lettering, I can spell it out. But the tag ... I can't read what's on it. It's all I have of Master. What did it say? Did it lead you back to Master?"

"It's too faded," Rayan admitted, and he saw the same emotions cross Sil's face as the ones he'd felt on that day.

"Oh," it breathed.

"But I can try again. If you'll allow me."

Sil glared at him. "Don't try to be all polite now. You've already read it."

"I'm just trying to make it right. Sil, I'm sorry."

Its glare softened as it let out a quiet sigh. Its hand dipped into its pocket and it fished out the tag, holding it close to its chest for just a brief moment before it handed it over to Rayan. "Anything you can make out is more than I have. If there's even just a letter, anything ... Maybe it'll jostle my memory. I don't know how much the medication took from me, I just know that it was a lot."

"I'll try my best," he promised as he gingerly took the tag again. "I can make out a capital B in the row that I think is meant to be your name."

"A B?" Sil's brows knitted together in concentration. "B ... My name, starting with a B ... Is there nothing more? How many letters, can you make that out?"

Rayan tried, but to no avail. "Maybe six? Or seven. There's an L in there, I think. Or is that an I? It's hard to say."

"B ... L ... What pet names are there with those letters? Don't you have – don't you have one of those books? Those pet name books? I remember seeing them at the facility."

Rayan perked up. "I have one! Wait here."

He rushed outside to retrieve it and noticed he'd left the TV on from earlier. There was a pet medication ad playing – or was it a pet medication ad? Rayan frowned in confusion, grabbing the remote and increasing the volume a bit.

"Mr. Barlowe, is there anything the public can do to help?"

It was Tarquin Barlowe, the man behind the famous pet med company. They sold vitamins or something; Rayan had looked into it more than once during the times he was daydreaming about owning a pet and giving it a good, proper life. Nutrition was a very important facet of keeping one.

"Just keep your eyes open, please. I have no idea what my precious Bubbles might look like after so much time without an owner, but I'm sure it's not good. Its characteristics are pale skin, brown eyes, brown hair ... It's also very tall, although the poor thing might

try to hide in small places. It is very traumatised. It might've also sustained some injuries while trying to find its way back. It's important that we find it as soon as possible so it can be properly cared for."

Bubbles? Tarquin Barlowe had lost a pet?

Wait a minute –

"Rayan?" Sil called from the bedroom.

Wait a minute …

"You heard it here, everyone. Mr. Barlowe is looking for a tall female pet with brown hair, brown eyes, and possible injuries it might've sustained while on the streets. Its name is Bubbles, but it might not respond to it right away, instead deciding to hide away from curious eyes and strangers. The best thing to do would be to call the PPA right away if you spot it."

B … L …

Bubbles.

Tarquin Barlowe had to be Sil's master. The kind master, the master from near the lake –

"Rayan?" Sil limped out into the living room with its crutches, its gaze finding the man on the TV screen. The remaining colour drained from its already pale cheeks. "Why is he there?" it stammered, tripping over itself in an attempt to get away. "Why – why is he – what is he doing there, why is he there?"

"Sil, love … Isn't that your master?" Rayan asked softly.

"No!" it screamed. "No! No! I won't go back! I won't be hurt again!"

"Sil, calm down, quiet – "

"I won't ever go back!"

"Sil!" Rayan rushed over, clamping a hand over its mouth. "Quiet! The neighbours will hear!"

Suddenly, Rayan's phone went off. He let it ring, focusing instead on stabilising his flailing little pet – when Sil *bit* him.

"Ouch!" he cried, pulling his hand back. "Sil!"

"I'm not going back!" It limped back to the bedroom, slamming the door shut with a loud *bang* that echoed through the small apartment. Rayan had no time to really digest what had just happened, he had to take the call from ... Dana?

He swiped his finger across the screen and muted the television. "Hello?"

"Hi."

Silence.

"Everything okay?"

Dana sighed on the other end. She sounded like she was on the verge of crying. "Can I come over?"

Rayan glanced towards the very much occupied bedroom. "Um ... Why? What's up?" He tried to sound as casual as possible, but he had a feeling that if Dana didn't suss out that something was wrong, it wasn't because of his acting skills. "Is everything okay?"

"Yes, um ... No, not really. Um ... " Rayan swore he heard a quiet half-sob. "I shouldn't be telling you this, but I can't really keep it a secret until the last moment, I guess ... Nima and Bo are expecting again."

Rayan almost dropped the phone. "What? You mean – Nima's pregnant?" Little Destin, Rayan's baby nephew, wasn't exactly a baby anymore; still, this was a stark reminder of the flow of time. "Right now? There's a baby on the way?"

"Yeah ... "

"But ... Wait, does that mean ... ?"

"The flat is small, even for the four of us. Nima and Bo ... they deserve a nice place to raise their kids. Without ... without me breathing down their necks. They're very nice about it, or they had been until now, um ... "

Oh no.

"Dana ... "

Another half-sob. "I didn't wanna trouble you with this, but ... "

Rayan swallowed. "Dana, I – "

"I know it's a lot to ask. I know."

She had no idea how much it was to ask. Why now? Why now, of all times, when he had a post-surgery illegal pet in his bedroom? But there was no way he could send her back to their parents' house. Not when ... not when they were the way they were. There was a reason they had all moved out as soon as possible.

"Please," Dana asked, voice small. "Can I move in with you?"

FIGURING IT OUT

"Dana, can we – can we talk later?"

"Please, Rayan, I know I'm asking a lot, but can I just come over? Just to talk it out? You don't have to decide right now, I'm just … I'm in a very sticky situation. Please, I just want to talk."

Rayan thought about Sil trembling under the covers. "I'm not at home right now," he lied, voice shaky.

"No? I thought – I thought your shift was already over?"

"I'm still at the supermarket."

"Oh … It's very quiet. I didn't realise. I'm sorry."

"We're definitely gonna talk, okay? You can come over on, um … " *Think fast. Think fast. Think fast.* "Tomorrow," he blurted out.

Stupid.

What was he going to do with Sil in a single day?

"Okay," Dana said, sniffling a little. "Thanks. I won't bother you. Just tell me a time and I'll come over. And please don't tell Nima that I told you. She said she wanted to keep it a secret for a bit longer."

"I won't tell her. I promise."

"Thanks. See you tomorrow, then."

Rayan hung up the phone and let out a sigh.

This was *not* good. Dana and Nima living together worked out just fine when the two of them were single; once Bo entered the picture, they'd had to make some compromises. But even with one kid, at least Dana could babysit ... but with another on the way, it was clear that Dana couldn't stay for much longer. Everyone had to know that.

But Nima wasn't going to just kick Dana out, right? With how nice she was, she would probably try to downplay it ... God, and Rayan was living all alone. Even though his apartment was a one-bedroom, it was very clear that the responsibility of letting his sister move in was now on him.

Later. He would think about this later. He had to check on Sil and figure out what this Tarquin Barlowe business was.

He tiptoed over to the bedroom door and gently knocked. "Love? Are you okay?"

"I'm not going back!" it yelled.

"Shh, please, keep your voice down!" He opened the door and quickly slipped inside, closing it behind himself and leaning up against it, as though that way he could prevent the PPA from busting through and taking him to prison and Sil to a shelter. "Please."

"You don't understand!" it said, flailing with its good arm. "You don't know what he did! He's the entire reason – he's the reason I'm like *this*!" It pointed to its leg, now in a cast. "He's the reason Master left me! No, I'm sure they didn't even leave me, I must've been stolen! He must've stolen me! He gave me the pills too! He did everything bad to me! Him and his sister and his other stupid pets!"

"Woah, woah, woah, slow down, calm down, quiet down … "

Sil pulled the blanket over itself protectively. "I'm never going back."

"Tarquin – the man on TV, he … he isn't your master? The master you love?"

"No!"

That didn't make sense. Barlowe owned a whole company dedicated to making pets' lives better … How … Why would he have so many pets if he was just going to treat them so badly? There was no way he could've done all that to Sil, right? But it seemed so sincere … and it had no reason to lie.

"Tarquin has a lot of pets," he tried cautiously. "All of them in pristine condition. His whole business is focused on the well-being of pets, he's under a microscope."

"Then that's why he never let me out," Sil growled. "Those other pets – they were paraded around. Happy. Content. They got regular meals and pretty clothes. I got scraps and the basement."

"You said he didn't even give you a name, but he said he was looking for a Bubbles."

Sil froze for a moment. "Bubbles," it said slowly, turning the name over in its mouth. "Bubbles ... Is that ... is that me?" It looked down at the tag in its hand. "Is that what Master named me?"

"Can I see that again?"

Sil hesitantly held it out for Rayan to take, and he inspected it once again, this time even more closely. "Yeah, I think that's Bubbles on here. I think that must've been your name."

"So why?" it asked, choked up. "Why did he never call me that? Why did he call me a mutt? A stupid thing? If I had a name, why was I only ever called bad names?"

Rayan's heart shattered at the sight. "Sil ... "

"Don't!" it snapped. "That's not my name! That's not my *real* name! That's a stupid, made-up name that I myself had to come up with! That wasn't what Master had named me!" It snatched the tag back and held it close to its chest, sobbing quietly. "Bubbles ... My name is Bubbles ... "

"I'm sorry," Rayan said clumsily. "I truly am. I ... I would've never guessed that Tarquin – god, it's horrible. He's ... he's so influential and – and such a big name in the industry, I looked up to him ... " Sil – Bubbles – looked at him like he was completely insane. "I thought he was a good owner. I thought he was a good *person*."

"Well, he's *not*."

Rayan's heart suddenly dropped. "And now he's after us," he breathed. "He has all the resources and connections in the world

... If he realises I have you and didn't report – holy shit, I'm in *huge* trouble."

Bubbles looked terrified at the prospect too. "What does that mean? *What does that mean*?" it demanded, more and more urgent. "That doesn't mean you'll report me and send me back, right? That can't be!"

"No, no, that's not – wait, *fuck*. Fuck, I didn't ask about the chip at the doctor's!" Rayan slapped himself on the forehead. There were too many things to keep in mind, too much happening all at once. "We need to get that chip out! We need to get it out before something happens! That's basically the only way they can reliably send you back to Tarquin, I think. We need another doctor's appointment."

"I have a chip?" Bubbles looked alarmed. "Where?"

"In the back of your neck. Every pet has one – it's to aid in identification."

"We have to get it out!" It put its good hand on the back of its neck, and for a moment, Rayan thought it might try to claw it out itself. "How do we get it out?"

"It's ... gonna be another surgery. But not right now. I mean, as soon as possible, but not right now. We're gonna have to deal with Dana as well ... God!" He buried his face in his hands, overwhelmed by this whole ordeal. "One thing at a time ... Just one thing at a time ... "

Bubbles grabbed him by the shirt. "Call the doctor!"

"I can't right now!"

"Why?"

"The last time I got a very specific window of time for when I could call her! She likely won't pick up! And we have a more urgent – or at least just as urgent matter to talk about." He put his hand on Bubbles', gently prying its fingers off. "My sister's visiting tomorrow. You're gonna have to hide for the duration of the visit; under the bed, or in the closet ... We'll figure something out. She's ... in need of a new place to stay, and the most realistic outcome is that I'm gonna be providing that place. I don't know how, yet, but um ... That's ... t hat's what's happening."

If possible, Bubbles looked even more alarmed. "You can't bring her here! You pushed me to have these surgeries, now I can't even run away, and now you want to bring someone here? A stranger?"

"It's gonna be fine," he hurried to assure it, though truth be told, he didn't know whether it would be fine. "I promise. It's gonna be fine. I'm gonna protect you. She's not moving in right away – we can probably try to find out more about your situation before then! You can be out of here and back with your nice, loving owner before push comes to shove."

If that loving owner was really a loving owner. If Bubbles was really right in assuming Tarquin somehow stole it ... however difficult that was to imagine.

"I'll try to secure a doctor's appointment for you as well. We'll figure this out. It's all going to be fine."

***

"Thanks for letting me come over," Dana said as she settled down on the sofa. Rayan had carefully hidden away all of Bubbles' clothes and cleared out a space for it in the closet – now it was just a matter of it not sneezing or coughing during her visit. The cramped space must not have been good for its post-op limbs either … They just had to make it quick. "I don't even know what I want to talk about, really … I mean … It's clear, isn't it? I've become a nuisance there. Nima would never say it, but that's how it is."

"Don't say that," Rayan said gently. "You're not a nuisance."

"I'm a nuisance here as well, aren't I?"

"No! No, not at all."

"It's just that … I don't think I can go back home. To Mom and Dad, I mean."

Rayan swallowed, trying not to say the wrong thing. He didn't know *what* to say. Their parents were … good people, really. It was just that they were a bit … strict. "I understand," he assured her. "I do."

"But you don't want me to move in."

"No! Dana, listen to me." He scooted closer, grabbing her hands and holding them between his own. "I love you, okay? We'll figure this out. I'm happy to have you stay here. It's just …

very sudden, yeah? We have a whole nine months to figure this out."

Achoo.

Rayan froze.

"What was that?" Dana asked, confused.

"The ... the neighbour," he stammered. "It – it really sounds like it was just like in the other room, huh? The curse of these apartments. Paper-thin walls. Um, back to Mom and Dad – "

"I can't go back to being slapped around," she blurted out. Rayan deflated at the mention of that. He hated thinking back to those times, before they had moved out. He hated to think that Dana might have to go back to that.

Maybe he should just come clean and introduce Bubbles and Dana. Maybe she would be understanding?

No, that was too risky. Too many variables.

"You won't have to," he tried to say as confidently as possible. "We'll make it work."

"I can pay you rent. I can ... maybe bring my bed over? Put it ... somewhere."

"We'll figure it out," he repeated for the thousandth time.

"You look ... a bit frazzled," she said with a chuckle. "Everything okay on your end?"

Oh, if she knew.

"Yeah. I'm just a bit shaken by all the new info. The new baby and all."

The conversation took a more pleasant turn, but Rayan couldn't push Bubbles out of the back of his mind. With every passing second he thought of it, all alone in that dark, cramped closet. By the time Dana was ready to leave, he couldn't be fast enough to let it out.

"She's gone," he said as he opened the door, and Bubbles slowly crawled out. "C'mere ... " He lifted it up in his arms, and the poor pet was too worn out to really protest. "It was a long time, wasn't it? I'm sorry. I didn't want to be rude."

"I'm tired ... " it muttered. "But the chip – can you call now?"

"Right. The chip." Rayan gently set it down on the bed and pulled out his phone. Just after six o'clock; maybe Dr. Anne would pick up.

"Do you think ... do you think there's a chance the chip belongs to Master? Not ... not my owner, but Master? Do you think there's a chance they didn't switch it out?" it asked. "Because, um ... I don't remember being chipped. Maybe ... maybe if my owner knew he wouldn't ever be letting me out of the basement, then he didn't feel the need ... "

For the first time in a little while, Rayan's heart leapt with hope. "It could be. Dr. Anne will surely help us figure it out."

Un-Chipped

This time, as Rayan was led into the doctor's office by Milo, he didn't even flinch at the way he glared at him. He was a lot less nervous and a lot more full of tentative hope – this chip might just prove to be the way to Bubbles' owner.

"Dr. Anne?" he called hesitantly once they reached the little office. "It's Rayan. I've come for the appointment."

"Yes, yes." She stepped out of an even smaller room with a gentle smile on her face, gesturing for the two of them to come closer. Even with the crutches, Bubbles needed some help to move comfortably. "Chip surgery, was it?"

"Um, first – "

"I want to know who I belong to," Bubbles cut in. "You can read this chip, right? Before you take it out? Or after. I don't care."

"You don't know?" she asked, a little surprised.

"I'm ... not sure. Maybe it's still in Master's name. I need to know."

Dr. Anne hummed. "That might be tricky. I don't really have access to the database, but we'll see what I can do. First things first, though, we'll get it out of you."

Bubbles swallowed audibly. "It's ... it's gonna be like last time, right? I'll be asleep?"

"No, no. We'll just inject you with a local anaesthetic."

It noticeably bristled at that. "No, I want to be asleep."

"We can't just put you to sleep for every procedure."

"It's gonna be fine," Rayan tried gently. "I'll be right here. You can hold my hand while she injects you."

Bubbles' eyes were darting between the two of them, glare deepening. "No. I don't like needles."

"Then you're not getting that chip out," Dr. Anne said, staring it down even stronger than it was staring her down. She spoke with authority, and Rayan was just about to cut in and try to ease the tension when Bubbles backed down.

"Fine," it muttered. It was gripping its crutches so hard its knuckles were white. "Do the stupid injection."

"I'll be right here the entire time," Rayan assured it again as he led it to the operating table. Bubbles lay on its stomach, its good hand in one of Rayan's. It was already squeezing. "You're gonna be okay, love."

"I just need to know whose chip is in me. I just – if there's any chance that it's Master's ... if I'm legally still Master's, with this chip, could I maybe go back to them?"

"I don't know your specific circumstances," Dr. Anne said as she was preparing the syringe. "That could be the case. But why wouldn't your new owner change the name on the chip?"

"Because he wanted to keep me a secret," it hissed. "That's why. I never saw a doctor, not after … not after he gave me the pills. I never saw a doctor at all, as far as I can remember."

"*He* gave you pills?" Dr. Anne raised an eyebrow. "That's sketchy. That's usually administered by the guys at the shelter or facility."

Rayan opened his mouth to say something, then closed it again. Right. Dr. Anne was right. How did he not catch that detail earlier? That must've been why Bubbles even remembered its previous owner. Master, as it called them. Tarquin must've somehow messed up the dosage or something – his business might've been a pet vitamin business, but he was a businessman, not a vet. "Is that even allowed?" he asked her.

"In some cases, yeah. If the client's a big shot."

Rayan bit the inside of his cheek. "It's Tarquin Barlowe," he blurted out. Dr. Anne stopped in her tracks.

"Come again?"

"It's Tarquin Barlowe. Bubbles confirmed it."

"Bubbles?" Recognition sparked in her eyes. "Right. He was on TV, looking for his lost pet. He never mentioned a chip. I knew there was something off about that announcement."

"Can we just get this over with before we start chatting?" Bubbles interrupted.

Dr. Anne chuckled. "Sure. I'm gonna inject you now, hold still."

Rayan had to look away as the needle was pushed inside, but he knew exactly when it hit skin; Bubbles' grip became ten times tighter, then it relaxed. "Is it still inside?" it asked hesitantly.

"Not anymore. Can you feel me poking you?"

"No."

"Good."

Bubbles didn't let go of his hand. "My neck feels weird."

"That's the anaesthetic working. Now, keep quiet. I need to focus so I don't cause you to be paralysed."

As Dr. Anne leaned over, Rayan caught a glimpse of ... a scar? There was a scar just above the collar of her shirt, right around the place where ... where she was marking Bubbles' neck to be cut into.

Rayan's eyes widened, but he didn't make a peep. He wouldn't until she was done with the surgery.

But that could only mean one thing, right?

No, there were many ways to obtain scars. There was no way the doctor was a pet. An ex-pet. Were ex-pets a thing outside of Pet Lib propaganda? His mind was reeling.

But all thoughts were pushed aside when he saw her take out the scalpel and put it at the base of Bubbles' neck. He immediately looked away.

"Squeamish, are we?" she asked teasingly and Rayan could only nod.

The seconds ticked by and Rayan waited, studying every pattern on the wall while he held Bubbles' hand. He didn't know how long it took to fish a chip out of someone's neck, and he didn't need to. That was where the professionals came in.

"Done," Dr. Anne said abruptly and Rayan looked back. The wound was all bandaged and – Rayan assumed – stitched up underneath. "I'll try to take a look and see who this chip belongs to and I'll give you guys a ring. How's that?"

"It's already out?" Bubbles blinked like a confused child. "I can get up?"

"Yeah, go on, go on. You're a free little critter now."

Bubbles pushed itself up and gently moved its neck, stretching it a little. "I'm ... free? What does that even mean? I don't want to be free. I want you to find who that chip belongs to and I want to go back to Master."

"All in due time."

"Dr. Anne – " Rayan interrupted quietly. "Can we have a word? Please? Just the two of us."

Bubbles narrowed its eyes at him. "About me?"

"No! No, I ... I mean, I guess it doesn't have to be just the two of us. If Dr. Anne's fine with a bit of a, um ... personal question about, um ... "

"I used to be a pet, yeah," she said easily. Rayan's eyes almost popped out.

"H-h   uh?"

Bubbles was similarly baffled. "What?"

"You saw my scar, didn't you?" She smiled and tapped the back of her neck. "That's where my chip came from. I ran and hid and studied medicine. Now I'm an illegal doctor – part-time, at least."

Rayan opened his mouth. Then closed it. Then opened it. Then closed it again. "How?" he managed to force out.

"You talked to the Pet Lib guys, arranged for a whole illegal doctor meeting, and you still believe in this pet bullshit? Hats off, you're blinder than I thought."

Rayan flushed deep red. "I don't understand," he said softly. "I'm sorry. I don't ... I don't get it. How ... how can a pet be a doctor? What do you mean you *used to* be a pet? If you're a doctor, shouldn't you ... shouldn't you especially believe in the system?"

"Get it together, boy. It's all smoke and mirrors." She snapped her fingers in front of his face a couple times, making him flinch. "Pets aren't a thing. We're all people."

Rayan frowned. "No, that's ... "

"That's not true," Bubbles said, and Rayan couldn't have been more grateful.

"But it is. Look around. Milo's an ex-pet too, I am an ex-pet, and tell you what – if I did the pet test on you right now, you'd probably be a pet."

That hurt. "That's not true!" he said desperately. "I'm a person! There's not a single pet in my family tree, that's stupid!"

"Wanna try it?" she asked with an insufferably smug grin, and Rayan couldn't turn it down.

"Yes. Let's try the test."

Bubbles didn't interrupt or ask to go home. As far as Rayan could see, it was just as curious to see the infamous test as he was. And the results.

Dr. Anne brought out a folder full of papers and sat down in the chair across from Rayan. "I'm going to say statements, you say whether they're true or false for you. First one: I am a person," she said in full seriousness. Rayan almost laughed.

"True."

"There are no pets in my family."

"True."

This was easy.

"I like being around pets more than people."

Rayan stopped for a moment and thought about his time spent volunteering at the local shelter. "Um ... " Okay, one wrong answer couldn't be too bad. Was it even the wrong answer? He didn't know. He didn't know much about this test, for all the faith he'd placed in it all his life. "True."

The statements went on. "*I get along with both of my parents.*" "*I have plenty of friends.*" "*Solving life's hardships comes naturally to me.*" "*People often scolded me as a child.*" Rayan soon found he felt he was answering incorrectly to most of them. He was squirming more and more in his seat.

"Congratulations," Dr. Anne said when they were finished. "You'd be cast as a pet. Don't ever let the PPA get their hands on you, you'll be memory wiped as soon as you set foot in that building."

"B-but – but there's a medical exam too – " he stammered. "They – they'd know – "

"The medical exam is complete bullshit," she said simply. "They check this, they check that, they write whatever's convenient based on this sample test. You were nervous the whole time too – that would get put down on paper as a sign that you're a pet as well. They'd spot you from a mile away. The only thing protecting your cushy little life right now is the fact that no one has reported you yet, and that you haven't been caught committing petty crimes."

"We're done here," Rayan snapped, standing abruptly. "Thank you for your help, Dr. Anne. I trust that Bubbles will heal well and we won't have to see each other again."

Dr. Anne smiled, softer than before. "Rayan ... listen to the people around you, yeah? They've had plenty of experience you'd do well to learn from."

"Thank you," he said curtly. "Goodbye."

Tragic Backstory

Thoughts were swirling inside Rayan's head at a rapid speed. What did that stupid sample test mean? He knew he wasn't a pet. Dr. Anne must've lied about the results to prove her point. But she didn't seem the type to do that ... As Rayan was helping Bubbles out of his sisters' car and into the building, he was too far away to even notice it talking to him.

"Rayan!" it snapped after a while, and Rayan was brought back to the present.

"Huh? Sorry, I – sorry. What were you saying?"

"What will you do now?"

"What do you mean?"

"You're so devoted to the system. Will you report to the PPA now? Let them take you? You can't leave me here alone. I won't let you. Not before the doctor tells me whose chip that was."

"Of course I won't report to the PPA," he said indignantly. "Whatever test that was, I'm sure it was just some made-up stuff. Dr. Anne wanted to convince me that pets didn't exist, so she made me out to be a 'pet' – but that doesn't mean anything. I don't have to report anything to anyone."

Bubbles nodded. "Okay. After I'm back with my real master, you can do whatever you want. But until then, no messing around with the PPA."

Rayan smiled at the way Bubbles tried to order him around, like ... like it was the owner and he was the pet. His guts churned at the notion.

If he had met Bubbles in any other circumstance, would he have mistaken it for a person? If Bubbles had met him in any other circumstance, would it have mistaken him for a pet? Was the line really so blurry?

Was the science behind it not as sound as he thought?

"Rayan!" Bubbles snapped its fingers in front of his face to get his attention. "What are you thinking about? That doctor didn't get into your head, did she? Pets exist – I'm living proof. Don't start believing all that crap, not now. Not before I'm out of here."

"Sorry. You're right." A pet ordering a person around ... They were an odd couple for sure, but that didn't mean Dr. Anne was right. "Let's get you back to bed so you can heal. I'll do some internet research about Tarquin, maybe something about your previous owner will pop up."

***

Rayan went down a rabbit hole of information about Tarquin Barlowe. He had a sister, Pandora Barlowe, with whom he'd started his company decades ago. The two of them had a lot of pets, which was to be expected – Bubbles was in none of the photos, though. As he researched more and more, he found several interviews Tarquin had given on the subject now that his pet was missing.

"I didn't want to expose it to the public given its shy demeanour and traumatising backstory," one article read. *"I realise now that if only I had taken at least a couple photos of it, this whole thing would be easier. It was just so reclusive and skittish, it didn't even occur to me ... To think that it's now out in the big wide world all alone, it breaks my heart."*

Traumatising backstory? "Bubbles?"

"Yes?" came the muffled reply from the bedroom. Rayan stood up, laptop in hand, and walked over there.

"I've been reading some articles, and Tarquin seems to always highlight some tragic backstory you had. Do you have any idea what he might be talking about?"

Bubbles made a face. "He stole me away from Master. That's tragic enough."

"I don't think he means that. He wouldn't be very public about that."

"I don't know ... I don't know. He gave me all those pills, they made me forget a lot of stuff. They made me forget the face of my master, their voice, their name ... I'm lucky I didn't forget about them entirely."

Rayan hummed. "Tragic backstory ... He never explicitly says what it is and I can't really find articles on it. I'll go back to looking."

Just as he was about to exit the bedroom, there was a knock on the door. He quickly pulled the bedroom door shut and put down the laptop on the coffee table, then went to open it.

"Who is it?"

"Pet Protection Agency."

Rayan froze. Again? They'd just been here a few days ago. "Uh ... Um ... " He opened the door, but he was unable to find the right words to express just how unwelcome this visit was. "Is this about the reports again?"

"I'm afraid so," the agent said. It was a woman, not much older than Rayan himself, who wore a uniform and a serious expression that made him wary. "I know my colleagues have been here not too long ago, but ever since then, we've gotten more reports about suspicious activity in the area. Can I come in?"

Rayan swallowed but stood aside, motioning for her to enter. She did so while observing everything in the flat, probably looking for clues. She seemed much more ruthless than the agent who had come before her. She seemed ... convinced this wasn't just a random report.

He could only hope Bubbles had already made it into the closet, into the little space that had been cleared out to serve as a hiding place.

"So, um ... what sort of report was it?" Rayan tried to ask nonchalantly.

"You live alone here, yes?"

"Yeah, just me."

"The neighbours keep hearing strange noises and even arguments."

Rayan kicked himself that he couldn't keep Bubbles more quiet. "Uh ... Yeah, that's ... Sometimes I have people over. Like my sister, Dana. She just visited. And sometimes I argue with my parents on the phone ... doesn't everyone? We don't have the best relationship – I won't go into details, if that's okay."

The woman regarded him with a suspicious look. "The neighbours said they never see anyone come or go."

Rayan furrowed his brows. "Well ... I don't assume they stand by their door all day, watching my flat. Right?"

The woman hummed. "I suppose not." She turned towards the bedroom door, and Rayan already knew he was going to be made to show her around. "Can I take a peek inside that room?"

"There's a bit of a mess there, but um ... sure. I mean, why not."

"I assure you, I'm not going to judge. The only thing I'm looking for is a stray pet. You must've seen the announcements about Mr. Barlowe's pet that's gone missing; we need to take reports much more seriously around this time."

Oh. So it was a money thing. Everyone wanted the reward that came with finding a millionaire's pet. "Of course. Bubbles, was it? It's deeply troubling." He led her to the bedroom door and tried to open it without much hesitation, hoping that Bubbles was already under the bed or in the closet.

Sure enough, the bed was empty.

"You use crutches?" the woman asked, immediately spotting the two that were laid against the bed.

"Y-y   eah. Yeah, I ... My legs are a bit ... weak, recently. The doctors don't know what's wrong with them – you see, I'm a waiter in the small Italian restaurant in town. I walk a lot, I have to be on my feet all the time. Anyway, I've been experiencing some muscle weakness, so they prescribed some mobility aids for me."

She narrowed her eyes at him but didn't pry. "I see. It must be hard."

Rayan could only nod with the lump in his throat. He thought if he said another word, he would immediately faint. He wasn't a good liar, or a good actor, or a good anything.

"Can I see the bathroom as well?"

"Yeah, of course. Right this way."

By some miracle, the woman found nothing amiss. By the time Rayan escorted her out and closed the door behind her, the nausea got so bad that he immediately had to rush back to the bathroom to retch.

"Fuck," he breathed. "Fuck. Fuck. They're onto us. They're so onto us. I can't do this."

He managed to get himself together enough to stumble back into the bedroom, quietly opening the closet door to find Bubbles huddled inside. It was looking up at him with big, tear-filled eyes – the poor thing must've been scared out of its mind too.

"She's gone," he whispered. "We have to be much more quiet from now on. The neighbours ... I don't know exactly what they're saying, but everyone's on high alert because Tarquin's lost a pet. They're taking reports much more seriously."

Bubbles nodded mutely. "I can't go back," it mumbled. "I can't – not when I'm so close. The doctor will find Master, I'm sure. I'm so close. Please, please, don't let them take me now. Don't let them take me back."

Rayan crouched down in front of it so they were at eye level. "I won't let them, love. I promise."

***

It was at least a week until Rayan got a call from an unknown number, and he took it with shaking hands. If it was the PPA again, he might not survive without a heart attack.

"Hello?" he almost squeaked.

"It's Dr. Anne," came the swift reply, and Rayan let out an audible sigh of relief. "What, were you expecting someone else?"

"It doesn't matter."

"It doesn't. Listen, I'm gonna be quick. I have good news and bad news: good news, the chip in Bubbles' neck really did have its previous owner's name attached. Wynn Havard."

"That's amazing – "

"Bad news is, Wynn seems to be dead."

ON THE RUN

It was like the rug had been pulled out from under Rayan. He had been carefully building a Jenga tower of questionable pieces, of surgeries and PPA visits and family conflicts, all to try and get Bubbles back to its owner … and its owner was dead. Wynn Havard was dead.

"Wh – what?"

"I can't talk much right now. I'm sorry, Rayan. I don't even know what Bubbles will say; try to be very patient with it. I have to go."

And she hung up.

Rayan collapsed onto his sofa, tears springing to his eyes. How was he meant to explain this to Bubbles? They'd been so close … He'd promised it'd be back with its owner before Dana moved in.

"Who was it?" came the question from the bedroom. Bubbles limped out with its crutches, looking at Rayan inquisitively. "Was it Dr. Anne? Did she find my owner?"

"It was in Tarquin's name," he said without thinking.

Bubbles stopped in its tracks, its face immediately falling. "Oh."

No, this wasn't right. It wasn't right to keep this information from it. Rayan took a deep breath and tried again. "Love ... Come, sit down."

"No, I ... I think I'm gonna go back to my room."

"Bubbles. Please."

Bubbles gave him a puzzled look but tentatively agreed, plopping down onto the sofa. "You said it was in my owner's name, what else is there to talk about? I get it. I'm not gonna freak out and start yelling. I'm gonna lay low until my limbs heal, then I can go out and find Master."

"I lied," he blurted out.

Bubbles looked even more perplexed. "What?"

"It wasn't in Tarquin's name. Bubbles, I – listen, please don't get mad at me. And please keep your voice down."

"What is it? What's going on?"

"Dr. Anne has found your master's name."

Bubbles' face lit up. "She has?"

"They're dead."

It was as though he'd punched it in the gut. Its face became distorted with pain beyond Rayan's understanding, and it slowly reached out to grab him by the shirt, pleading without words.

Please, tell me you're lying.

"I'm sorry," Rayan whispered.

"They can't be dead," it muttered. "They can't be. What are you even saying? This is stupid. Dr. Anne is stupid. What was their name? Let me look for them, I'll find them – "

"Their name was Wynn Havard."

"*Is* Wynn Havard."

"Bubbles – "

"Don't. Don't call me that." It let go and leaned back, tears now freely pouring down its face. "Don't. Don't say anything. I don't want to hear it. This is wrong. You're all wrong."

"You said you didn't think your master gave you up, and yet you somehow ended up with Tarquin. That, coupled with the fact he's saying you're highly traumatised – "

"He's saying that because he abused me!" it snapped.

"Keep your voice down," Rayan said, pleading. "The PPA – "

"I don't care about the PPA!"

"Please, Sil – "

"Don't call me anything! I'm leaving! I'm gonna go find Master! Wynn, I'm gonna find them, I'm gonna – "

Rayan grabbed it by the good arm and pulled it into a hug, holding it tight. He could feel it sobbing against his shoulder as it eventually gave up struggling, wrapping its thin little arms around him. "I'm sorry."

"I can never go back to being Bubbles?" it choked out, and Rayan tried to keep his own tears to a minimum. "I can never go back to having a loving home? I can never go back to … before?"

"I'm sorry," he repeated. "I'm so, *so* sorry."

"Where do I even go from here?"

"I don't know ... "

"I can't stay here. The PPA will hunt me down. You'll go to prison, I'll go back to my stupid owner – "

"We'll figure something out."

"What?" it snapped again. "Your sister wants to move in too – it's all a mess! I can't stay here, but I have nowhere to go!"

"Shh ... " Rayan rubbed its back in circles, trying to soothe it. "It's okay. I mean, it's not ... But we're gonna figure it out."

In truth, Rayan had no idea what to do. He was already eating through his savings trying to keep the two of them afloat, especially with the illegal doctor's visits. The PPA was clearly increasing their security checks. Nima's baby was on the way.

Sil pushed him away, crossing its arms and looking absolutely defeated. "I ... Maybe I should just give myself up."

"No, no, Sil ... "

"What's the point? My owner was right – there's no one coming for me. He'll make up some story about how I injured myself while on the run and he'll get off scot-free. I'll go back to being a punching bag."

"That can't be the only solution! That's no solution at all! What if I went with you to the PPA and explained – "

"They won't believe you."

Rayan frowned. "But ... but they're called the Pet Protection Agency ... They're supposed to protect pets like you ... "

Sil scoffed. "Grow up. They've never protected anybody."

"Don't take this as an insult, but I think we'll see each other a lot more in the future. You seem like a pretty good guy, and if you're going about this the illegal way, you'll very quickly realise that we might not be the cultists here."

"Listen to the people around you, yeah? They've had plenty of experience you'd do well to learn from."

Denice and Dr. Anne's words echoed in his mind, making him dizzy. If the PPA was corrupt, if Tarquin was lying on live television, if his neighbours were constantly reporting suspicious activity, if he didn't even trust his own family to have his back in this sketchy situation, then ...

"I'm gonna go back to Pet Lib," he exclaimed. "They'll know what to do."

***

"Leave the country."

Rayan recoiled. Denice was sitting across from him at a small table, looking deathly serious. "What?"

"If you really want to protect that poor guy, you'll help it leave the country. You'll go somewhere where pets are outlawed."

"I can't do that! I have all my family here, my savings, I – "

"Rayan." Denice leaned over the table. "Your window of opportunity is very quickly closing. They're cracking down on us all around the country because Tarquin has lost his pet – I'm not even gonna ask whether that's the same pet you keep in your flat. If you truly want to help, and you want us to be able to help you in return, you'll leave *right now*."

Rayan left the room more disoriented than he'd gone in. He couldn't just leave. Leaving his parents behind – that was long overdue. But his sisters? Bo? Little Destin? There was no way.

As he neared his apartment, he noticed a van parked in front of the building.

Pet Protection Agency.

His heart skipped a beat.

Sil.

"Rayan!" someone hissed from behind and he spun around, finding a very dishevelled Sil motioning for him to follow into an alleyway. He quickly dove behind the wall, just as a few agents exited the building. "They almost got me," it explained in a hushed voice. "We can't go back inside. Or at least I can't – but I heard them mention some arrest warrant."

"Oh god," he breathed.

"We need to leave. I brought some food along, maybe we could go to your family – "

"We can't. What if we get them into trouble too?"

Sil frowned. "So then what? Do you wanna live behind dumpsters with me?"

"I ... I don't know, can't I just go talk to them?"

"Rayan, they're out to *get you*."

Rayan shivered. He never wanted this. He just wanted to help. "Okay. We'll take a shortcut and go to my sisters' place. Can you keep up with those crutches?"

"If my life depends on it, yeah. I told you: I'm *not* going back."

***

Rayan almost collapsed into Dana's arms when she opened the door. "Please, help," he whined. "Please ... please, I'm in so much trouble."

"Who is it?" Nima called from the living room.

"What's going on?" Dana asked.

Sil was standing behind him, holding on to his shirt like it was scared that at any moment Rayan's sisters might turn on it. "We'll explain when we're inside," it said hurriedly. "Just let us in."

"Who is that?"

"Let us in," Rayan pleaded and Dana stepped aside. Sil hurriedly waddled inside.

"Rayan?" Nima came out with Destin following in tow, quickly wrapping a towel around her hair to keep it out of view of strangers, her eyes widening as she took in the sight in front of her. "Who is that?"

"Sil – Bubbles – Tarquin Barlowe's lost pet, but he kept it a secret and abused it, it can't go back, we need a place to stay, the PPA wants to arrest me – "

"Woah, hey, okay, what lost pet?"

"Don't tell them!" Sil snapped.

"I have to!" Rayan sobbed. He couldn't keep it in anymore. He was in shambles. "Dana, you can have the flat, I need to leave the country! The Pet Lib people said I need to – and – and I don't wanna go to jail, I ... I have to somehow leave – and I can't stay here, they'll arrest you too – "

Through effortful half-sentences told between sobs, Rayan finally managed to get the story together. His sisters were both horrified at the state of affairs and Sil was furious that he'd just told everyone, but there was no going back now.

"This will likely be the first place they'll look for me," Rayan finished in tears.

"We'll just go on the run while they get us fake papers," Sil said. "You said they can get us fake papers, right?"

"Don't be silly," Nima tried gently. "This is all so silly. All you have to do is give Sil to the PPA, and they'll handle everything."

"No!" Sil snapped.

"I can't," Rayan said as well. "I – I'm not sure about this pet thing anymore – "

"I'm sure about the pet thing, but the PPA is useless!"

Dana motioned for them to keep it down. "Okay, okay, what about this? I'll go look after your flat until you can send Sil on its way, and then you can just come back. How's that?"

"You need to tell me whether they really want to arrest me," Rayan begged. "Please. Please, you can stay there for as long as you want, just please, tell me. I'd love to come back – I'm just not sure I can."

"We talked enough," Sil said gruffly. "Let's go before the PPA comes."

"But the PPA is the authority in this case," Nima said, still apprehensive. "This is madness. Rayan, you can't possibly be going *on the run*. What would our parents think? What about your job?"

"It was a mistake to tell them," Sil cut in.

"No, Sil, they'll help – "

"We'll help," Dana assured him. "Nima, please take Destin back to the bedroom. I'll go with Rayan to his apartment. We'll figure it out. If the police come here, don't say *anything*."

"This is madness! Dana, you can't seriously be telling me that!"

"We have to go. *Now*." Sil grabbed Rayan by the hand and shoved him towards the door. "Bye. If the PPA comes after us, we'll know who told them where we are. So don't. Say. *A word*."

With that, the three of them left.

SMOKE AND MIRRORS

Things were not looking good.

Through Dana, Rayan quickly figured out that there really was an arrest warrant out for him. His parents were apparently more than happy to work with the police and the PPA, eager to seem like good, upstanding citizens of a country still so foreign to them after decades.

"It's not good," Dana whispered into the phone one night. Rayan was huddled close to a very protective Sil, using the last of his phone's battery power on a call with his sister. "Dad said – I don't even want to repeat what Dad said. But the flat is okay, I put everything back in place for you. Um … are the two of you okay?"

"I'm cold all the time," Rayan said quietly. "And scared. There are agents around every Pet Lib place, we'll … have to find another way to contact them. Dana, I'm so sorry."

"You have nothing to apologise for. You were dragged into this – maybe it wasn't the best decision to keep an illegal pet, but we understand. Mom and Dad, not really, but ... me, Nima, and the others. We understand."

"I don't think there's a way around it," he muttered. "I think I really have to leave. The country, I mean. I think there's no other choice."

"Rayan ... "

"I ... I'm never gonna open that dessert shop, huh?" He let out a small, miserable, humourless chuckle. "To think my life was normal up until a few weeks ago, and now it's come to this ... "

"It will go back to normal, love," Dana insisted. "I – "

"Hang up," Sil hissed. "There's someone coming."

"Dana, I have to go," Rayan said quickly.

"Wait – "

"I'll call you back!"

He hung up before she could've said anything, and both of them pressed themselves up against the wall of the alley. Rayan could hear the quiet buzz off the phone in his pocket as it powered off. He wasn't going to call her back.

"It's not the PPA," Sil whispered. "Just some guys."

"You lived like this for a whole year?" Rayan asked, bewildered. "I – this is horrible ... "

Sil shot him a look. "Well, get used to it. If you don't, I'll just leave you behind."

That wasn't an option. Sil still needed crutches to move around – the two of them could only survive on the streets together.

"What if we went to Dr. Anne? She would be able to connect us with the Pet Lib guys."

"Fine. Just follow my lead. We have one big advantage, and that's that pets look just like people. *Don't* look suspicious or nervous. If you walk confidently, they'll never be able to tell."

Confidence. That wasn't something Rayan had ever possessed, especially not since the day his girlfriend had broken up with him publicly. This was a matter of life and death, though, so he straightened his back and followed Sil across the street.

No one batted an eye.

The only thing protecting your cushy little life right now is the fact that no one has reported you yet, and that you haven't been caught committing petty crimes.

Was this whole thing really one big sham? Smoke and mirrors? Was he no different to Sil? Were the two of them no different to the guys on the other side of the street, having fun?

They didn't seem to be. No one called the PPA on them as they walked into another alleyway that would lead them to Dr. Anne's office.

"You're doing better than expected," Sil said, and Rayan felt like that was the most he was going to get as far as compliments went. "We'll sleep behind that dumpster. Maybe *in* the dumpster, depends on the temperature."

Rayan wrinkled his nose. "I'm not – "

"That, the police, or freezing to death. Pick your poison."

He sighed. "Let's just try our luck outside first."

As they settled down, Rayan realised just how hungry he was. He hadn't eaten in at least a day, when he and Sil had shared a pack of biscuits. Even though it'd only been a good twenty-four hours, Rayan could see why Sil became so protective of even the mush he'd unknowingly fed it.

"Seriously," he said quietly. "How did you do this?"

"It's not even that bad," Sil groaned. "Quit whining so much."

"And your ankle was busted too – "

"*Quit whining.*"

Rayan's mouth snapped shut. It would've been funny how quickly the roles were reversed, had it not been absolutely tragic.

After a few minutes of silence, Rayan could hear quiet sobbing. When he looked up, it was too dark to make out Sil's face, but he could see the outline of its shoulders rising and falling with each choked breath.

"Sil ... "

"Don't."

Another few minutes passed, and Sil abruptly scooted closer.

"For warmth," it mumbled, and Rayan had a feeling he would've been reprimanded for pushing it.

They stayed like that for hours, dozing off every now and then. Rayan could only praise and give thanks to whatever higher power was out there that he didn't need to go through this alone.

***

It took three days for Dr. Anne to show up to the illegal clinic. In those three days, the two of them had lied, cheated, and stole, trying to evade both PPA and police in their quest to stay alive and safe. Sil caught a glimpse of her and immediately alerted Rayan, then instructed him to walk over there and go inside with her. It'd follow in a few minutes, it had said.

"It'd look too suspicious if we approached her all at once," it explained. "Go. I survived out here for a year, you couldn't handle five minutes on your own."

Rayan got to her just before she closed the door. "Dr. Anne?"

"Rayan? I thought – oh lord, where's Bubbles?"

"Can I come in? Please? I'll explain – "

"You're asking me to hide a criminal."

"You're a criminal yourself!" he said desperately. "Please? Please, I won't make a peep."

Dr. Anne sighed and opened the door wider, letting Rayan slip inside. "Where's Bubbles?"

"It goes by Sil again. Ever since ... the news."

"Oh."

"It's hiding out in the alley next to the clinic. It said it would follow in a few minutes, but that it didn't want to cause a commotion."

Dr. Anne pushed up the glasses on her nose. "Well, you two have caused *quite* the commotion. Out of every runaway, did you have to find Tarquin Barlowe's? He's offering an insane reward for whoever brings you two to justice, you know. I could get rich and never look back."

Rayan's blood turned to ice in his veins. "You – you wouldn't – "

Dr. Anne waved him off. "Of course I wouldn't. I'm just saying, you're very lucky."

"So we can stay here a while? Just – we'll be gone in a minute. We just need to ask something of you. Please."

There was a knock on the door and Milo went to go get it, ushering a rough-looking Sil to the centre of the room. "We need your help," it said curtly.

"I can see that. All this running around isn't very good for those bones, is it?"

Sil scoffed. "Whatever. We need you to bring us to the Pet Lib people without them seeing. Or bring the Pet Lib people to us."

"Quite demanding, aren't you?" She sat down in one of the chairs and motioned for Rayan and Sil to take the other two. Milo stood guard at the door. "You two are *very* lucky that I decided to put my life on the line every day to help people just like you."

"So you'll help?" Rayan asked, leaning forwards. "You'll help us?"

"I'll do what I can."

"Um ... " Rayan averted his gaze, fidgeting with the hem of his shirt. "Do you think ... Would there be a way for me to ... to stay here? Maybe put Sil on a boat – "

"You can't stay in a country where Barlowe has such a reach," Dr. Anne said without hesitation. Rayan deflated.

"I see."

"It's only fair," Sil muttered. Dr. Anne said nothing, eyeing Rayan cautiously, probably waiting for him to blow up.

He didn't. Sil was right – it had lost everything, it was only fair that Rayan would now lose it all too. Or, well ... maybe not fair, but ... something close to it. Rayan wished there was another way, but he also couldn't fault Sil for any of it.

"Just ... please connect us with the Pet Lib guys. That's the last thing we'll hopefully ever ask of you," Rayan said quietly. "And I'm sorry I ran away like that last time. I was ... I was running from a lot of things. I'm really grateful for all you've done for us."

Dr. Anne rewarded his heartfelt apology with a gentle smile. "You're doing the right thing, you know. You just have to persevere. You both do. I'll see what I can do on my end."

— · —

COMRADE

"We need to stay alert," Sil said, sitting on Dr. Anne's operating table and glaring at a very sleepy Rayan who was about to doze off in a chair. "You can't just let yourself go like that."

"We're safe for now," he tried. Sil made a face.

"We don't know that. We barely know her intentions."

"She's an ex-pet who's probably also on a couple hit lists. She won't sell us out."

"*We don't know that.*"

"Sil, please ... "

It slapped Rayan in the upper arm with its good hand. "Stay awake," it hissed. "If we have to run, we run together. Isn't that what you promised me? Isn't that what you said we would do? I can't keep looking after you all the time, I need you to pull your weight."

"I looked after you for – "

"I know!" it snapped. "I know, and now I'm looking after you! Why won't you just make it a bit easier for me?"

"As if you ever made it easy!" he yelled back. "As if you ever considered my stance! My situation!"

"Oh, don't try to play the victim."

Rayan let out a frustrated sigh. "I *am* a victim. I left everything behind to help you!"

"You left everything behind to run from the police," Sil shot back. "Don't try to make yourself out to be a martyr. You're just as selfish as I am, but you could at least be grateful that I stole some food for you. Without me, you'd be rotting in a cell and eating whatever they gave you."

"Maybe that'd be better than sitting here with *you*."

Sil recoiled at the sharp words, its mouth snapping shut. It blinked a few times, giving Rayan enough time to massage his temples and try to collect himself.

"I'm sorry, I didn't mean – "

"Okay." Sil leaned back against the wall, crossing its arms. "Fine. I don't care. Do you think I care? Go and give yourself up for all I care."

"Sil … "

"Shut up. I guess I should be grateful that you finally showed your true colours."

Rayan wanted to respond, but all that came out was a choked little sob. He didn't mean to say that. He was just angry. "Sil," he whimpered, tears trickling down his cheeks. He couldn't say any more before the floodgates fully opened and he dissolved into a wailing mess.

"Fuck," Sil breathed. "Stop that. *Stop*."

He couldn't. All he could do was bury his face in his hands, tears falling onto the ground below and collecting into a little puddle. He was a mess. He was hungry, he was scared, he was cut off from his family, and he snapped at Sil and said some things he hadn't fucking meant to. Sil was all he had. If he lost it, what would he even do?

Suddenly, two thin little arms were wrapped around him, enveloping him in a warm hug. He threw his arms around the other, pulling it close and sobbing into the crook of its neck. "I'm sorry," he cried. "I'm sorry, Sil, please, I'm sorry, I just wanna go home ... I just want this all to be over ... "

"It'll be over," it said gently. "It will be. At some point, one way or another, it will be over. I'm ... " It took a deep breath, rubbing his back a little. "I'm sorry too. I've said some things ... Whatever. You know what I mean."

He did. And he was grateful.

When Dr. Anne came back, she found them still hugging it out, clinging to each other like two people who really had no one else in the world on their side. Thankfully, that didn't seem to be the case.

"They're ready for you," she said with a smile. "So stop the pity party."

"Sorry," Rayan said, wiping his face. Sil also returned to scowling as soon as the two of them separated, and Rayan found he much preferred that to its teary little face from before. "Who are 'they', exactly?"

"Denice and the guys. I let them know you two need a temporary place to stay – I didn't need to explain much. They watch the news too; they know your exact situation, like everyone else in Laka. Maybe the whole of Lezune."

Rayan glanced at Sil. Sil glanced back at him. "But we'll be safe there, right?" it asked, looking back at Dr. Anne. "They can keep us safe?"

"You won't even have to go outside," she said with a grin. "Hop off the operating table."

Sil did so and Milo immediately stepped up to push the table to the side. Dr. Anne grabbed a handle Rayan hadn't noticed until then, pulling part of the floor aside to reveal an underground tunnel.

"Woah," he said softly. "Was that there the whole time?"

"No, we just dug it yesterday," Dr. Anne said sarcastically. "How do you think I go in and out of this building? I can't be seen entering any place too many times or they'll come investigate it. Come on, jump down."

Rayan was the first to enter the tunnel so he could then help Sil land softly enough on its ruined ankle with the crutches. They said their goodbyes to Dr. Anne, who only sent Milo with them to show the way.

"I can't believe I never noticed that," Rayan marvelled.

"You never notice anything," Sil retorted. "I'm not too surprised."

"Quiet," Milo hissed. "We're below a pretty quiet street, we don't need them finding out there's a tunnel underneath."

Rayan clamped a hand over his mouth. "Sorry."

The journey was pretty much smooth sailing until they reached another trap door. Milo knocked on it in a specific pattern and it was soon opened, and Rayan found himself staring straight at a smugly grinning Denice.

"What's up, comrade?"

Rayan thought back to the way he'd criticised Pet Lib and Denice's vocation and blushed deep red. How the world had changed in just a few weeks.

He climbed out with Milo, then the two of them helped Sil get up. They were in some sort of cellar with a bunch of people around, or ...

"Is everyone here an ex-pet?" Rayan asked quietly. Denice's grin widened.

"Why don't you try and guess?"

"We don't have time for stupid games," Sil growled.

"No, no, I think this is quite an important game. Go on. Guess who's an ex-pet."

Rayan looked around and realised the task was impossible. Everyone looked like an ex-pet to him, mostly because everyone looked like an enemy of the state. Who else would rebel against a system if not ex-pets? "Um ... I ... Uh ... "

Fuck.

Denice clapped him on the shoulder. "Yeah, exactly."

"B-but pets look like people – "

"Because they *are* people, silly."

Rayan looked around again, trying to make sense of a reality that was rapidly shifting from second to second.

"You look like an ex-pet right now too," a woman said from the corner. "Are you?"

"No! No, I'm ... I look like an ex-pet ... ?"

She shrugged. "You look rough enough to have been abused by a bad owner. I looked much the same when I escaped."

"We don't have *time* for this," Sil said again. "You." It pointed at Denice. "Help us get out of here. Out of my owner's reach. Out of this stupid country."

"We're working on your fake papers now," Denice assured it. "You're gonna have to stay put for just a bit longer. Don't worry – this place is safe."

***

Through talking, Rayan learned that at most half the people in that cellar were actually ex-pets. *People*. They were all people, the lot of them. There was no way for him to differentiate between people from facilities and normal homes, and while Sil seemed especially opposed to the idea that the system was built on lies, Rayan was believing it more and more.

"You failed a pet test?" he asked one of the men – Axel – absolutely horrified. "So they took you away from your parents? I mean, I knew that was a thing, I just ... "

"Yup. They didn't do a damn thing to protect me." He pulled his shirt collar aside to reveal a similar scar to Sil's. "They put a chip in me first thing to prevent me from escaping. Apparently the one I had functioned as a tracker – someone paid good money to have me be processed. Have you heard of 'custom pets'? The sick fucks at the top can have people be abducted and processed into the system."

"There's no way ... "

"Oh, but there is. They pay the PPA to have people be turned into slaves, they pay the PPA to leave them alone as they abuse them, they pay the PPA to turn a blind eye when those pets suddenly disappear one day ... I'm not saying everyone at every level knows what's going on, but I'm sure as hell saying the top fuckers know."

"Rayan, Sil," Denice called as she descended the stairs. "We've got your papers. Get your things together and let's go."

"R-right now? Like, immediately?"

Sil didn't seem to have such hang-ups. It grabbed its backpack and stood up, pulling the crutches under its arms. "Let's go. Don't tell me you were still holding on to the notion that we might be able to stay."

Sil's vehement objections to befriending any of the people here suddenly seemed to make a lot more sense. Rayan let out a defeated sigh and followed it up the stairs.

"It's the dead of night, but you never know," Denice said as she fitted Rayan with a beanie and an eye-patch. "Your face is all over the news. Change into these clothes."

Sil was given different clothes as well – a dark blue jacket instead of its regular red one that had become iconic in the past days, dark pants to match, and even a wheelchair.

"You can lift it, right?" Denice asked. "You'll need to lift it into the boat when you get to the shore. There'll be new crutches for you on the ship, but you can't use them until then. Everyone is on the lookout for a pet with crutches."

Sil swallowed. "So I'll just have to rely on Rayan pushing me around?"

"For a little while." Denice shot it an apologetic smile. "He's trying his best. Give him a chance."

"One chance is *all* I have."

"All *we* have," Rayan amended quietly. "I promise, I'm in it as much as you are. I won't mess up."

Sil hesitantly gave up its crutches and sat in the chair. Rayan exchanged goodbyes with all his new friends and, lastly, Denice.

"I knew you'd come around," she said with a warm smile. "And hey, if you get caught, rest assured that we have a small, radical team on our side, specialising in busting out people from prison."

Rayan let out a small chuckle, shocked at the surreal idea. "Thanks, Denice. Well ... this is goodbye, then."

"It's just see you later. We'll get pets outlawed here sooner or later, and you guys will be welcomed back with open arms. Just you wait."

He didn't want to say it, but Rayan knew there was a very small chance of that happening. Not with most of the revolutionary action taking place across the ocean, where they were now headed. "Yeah. I'll be waiting."

"Let's go," Sil said gruffly, and Rayan immediately put his hands on the handles of its wheelchair.

"Right. See you later."

THE SHIP THAT SAILED

The streets were dark and quiet as the two of them followed the path set out by Denice and the others. They were going through narrow alleyways and streets barely illuminated by the streetlights, getting closer and closer to the ocean. Rayan could already smell it. It wasn't too far now.

"Hey," someone yelled from across the street and Rayan froze.

"Don't stop," Sil whispered. "Go. Go, go, *go*."

"Hey, you!"

Rayan couldn't will his legs to move. He swallowed thickly as he turned to meet the gaze of the man shouting at him, hoping he didn't look as suspicious as he felt. "Yes?"

"There's a curfew order in place, didn't you hear?"

Curfew?

Denice hadn't said anything about a curfew.

"N-no, I'm sorry." As the man got even closer, Rayan got to take a good, close look at the PPA badge on the front of his uniform. "I was just taking my sister out for some fresh air," he tried as nonchalantly as possible. "It – " *Fuck*. "She gets very sick sometimes if she has to lie down for a long period of time. She gets these asthma attacks – we were just going to the shore for – "

Sil suddenly stood up, balancing on its one good leg. Rayan's eyes widened as he watched it gain momentum and –

Bang.

It smacked the guy across the head with the cast on its bad arm, wincing as the healing bones took the impact. The PPA agent was out cold.

"You can't just do that!" Rayan whisper-screamed as Sil sat back down.

"Go," it hissed. "Come on. Go!"

Rayan couldn't stay calm anymore. He raced down the streets with all the stamina he had, grabbing Sil and holding it in a bridal carry once they reached the sandy shore, where the wheelchair became quite useless. There was a little boat waiting for them, according to Denice.

But where?

"There it is!" Sil suddenly said, pointing to a shadow on the water.

"Hey! You there! Stop!" someone yelled. Rayan ran even faster. "*Stop!*"

Sil buried its face in his chest as the two of them rushed to the boat, almost not wanting to let go when Rayan basically threw it on one of the benches. "Row!" it screamed in a panicked frenzy.

"I'm on it!" Rayan shouted back, trying to push the boat onto the water. He could hear the man running across the sand to catch up to them, and he pushed with all his might, trying his best to get out of reach.

"Stop immediately! You're under arrest!"

Rayan jumped into the boat and grabbed the paddles, rowing as fast as he could. The two of them started gaining momentum as he did so, leaving the PPA agent behind.

Sil let out a relieved sigh, carding through its sweat-damp hair with its good hand. "Fuck," it breathed.

"Fuck indeed," Rayan agreed quietly, still rowing like his life depended on it.

Because it kind of did.

When the two of them caught a glimpse of the promised ship in the distance, even Rayan started to feel the knots in his stomach loosen. It was floating in place with the anchor down, and they went up to it as close as safely possible.

"They're here!" someone on board yelled, and the lifeboat was soon lowered. Rayan helped Sil into it before climbing over himself, and then the two of them were pulled up, both utterly exhausted from the cat and mouse chase they'd just endured.

"We did it," Rayan panted on the floor. For the first time in all their days together, he saw Sil *smile* as he looked over.

"We did it!" it said, more enthusiastic. "We did it! We're out! We're out!"

Rayan sat up and looked over the railing into the ocean, thinking about the family he was leaving behind. "We did it ... "

Sil crashed into him for a big hug, holding on tighter than ever. "We did it," it whispered. "I never have to be hurt again. I – I'll miss Master more than anything, but we ... we did it. I'm sorry about your family. But we did it. We're out."

Rayan hugged back, more aware than ever that they were all each of them had. "We did it."

***

"Rayan!" Silja yelled as it barged in through the front door. "Rayan!"

"What?" he yelled back from the kitchen, putting a freshly baked batch of muffins on the counter and pulling off his oven mitts.

Instead of answering, Silja rushed into the kitchen with a wide grin on its face, holding a piece of paper in front of its now-less-scrawny body. Rayan immediately knew what it was – the only thing that had mattered in these last few days.

"You graduated?" he asked with a grin now matching Silja's, taking the paper from its hands. "You scored ninety-eight out of one hundred! Sil, that's outstanding!"

Silja threw its hair back and twirled around, then bowed with great flourish. "That's Silja for you."

"We're celebrating today, then! I knew you'd do it, love. I've prepared some muffins for you!"

The two of them sat down at the kitchen table, and after they'd let the muffins cool for a while – and Rayan had taken a sufficient amount of pictures of Silja's graduation papers – they began to eat.

"I told you I could do it," Silja said with its mouth full of delicious, chocolatey goodness.

"I never doubted you," Rayan responded with a warm smile.

"You would've doubted me way back when! When you thought I was just a dumb pet!"

Rayan reached over and ruffled its hair, making Silja laugh and swat his hand away. "You'll never stop bringing that up, will you?"

"Never ever."

Rayan looked back at the piece of paper proving that Silja was now a high school graduate and found that one particular detail warmed his heart more than even the incredible score written on the front. Tears sprung to his eyes as he took it in, and he tried his best to wipe them away as discreetly as possible.

Silja Kamali.

As much as he missed his family abroad, there was always a little sister here for him to be proud of.

ABOUT THE AUTHOR

Zi Trone is but a humble fear enthusiast with a passion for writing. An undying love for scared and crying characters has been the driving force behind hundreds of thousands of words already written, and hopefully many more to come.

— · —

Before You Go

This is the tenth book in 12 Months of Whump, a series of whumpy novellas published by WPP throughout 2025. Each novella can be read as a standalone.

To stay up to date with the 12 Months of Whump series and other whumperfly-inducing projects, visit us at https://thewhumpyprintingpress.tumblr.com/